DOC
CHRISTMAS
and
The Magic of Trains

A Novel By

NEIL ENOCK

www.neilenock.com

www.itinkr.com

Copyright © 2015 by Neil Enock

Itinkr Inc.
224 - 2nd Avenue N.E.
Calgary, Alberta, Canada, T2E 0E2
www.itinkr.com

Ordering Information:
Quantity sales. Special discounts are available on quantity purchases by corporations, associations, and others. For details, contact the publisher at the address above.
Orders by bookstores and wholesalers. Please contact iTinkr Inc.:
Tel: (877) 578-9771; Fax: (877) 509-1771 or visit www.itinkr.com.

Printed in Canada

Library and Archives Canada Cataloguing in Publication

Enock, Neil, 1957-, author
        Doc Christmas / Neil Enock.

ISBN 978-1-988108-00-1 (Case bound)
ISBN 978-1-988108-04-9 (Trade paperback)
ISBN 978-1-988108-02-5 (Electronic Book)

        1. Christmas--Fiction. I. Title.

PS8609.N667D62 2015   C813'6   C2015-906188-1

First Edition

14 13 12 11 10 / 10 9 8 7 6 5 4 3 2 1

To Suzanne and my family
for all the time I spent 'away' writing...

To my mother, who
always said I could do anything,
and who gave me a train set
when I was a boy...

To Allan Stickel and all of my friends
who first heard the story, and
encouraged me to continue...

To Simon Rose, whose skill as
an Editor you would most definitely
appreciate if you saw the first draft...

To all those who enjoy the
magic of the season at
Christmas...

And

to people of all ages
who understand
...the magic of trains!

- Neil Enock

CHAPTER 1

Searching

Darkness took over as the glow slowly faded behind them. Nick paused as he looked down from the last step of the train onto the darkened platform. It seemed to be covered in a smooth unbroken layer of snow.

"Snow?" said Marco, as he curiously peered over Nick's shoulder. "There can't be snow."

He impatiently pushed past Nick. As he jumped down from the train, he tripped and landed face first. Clouds of fluffy, soft particles rose up all around him, lingering in the air in exactly the same way that snow doesn't. Marco sneezed and coughed and then sneezed again.

Nick couldn't help but grin as he carefully stepped down from the train and helped Marco to his feet.

"Not snow." he said. "Dust."

As their eyes became adjusted to the dim light they

began to examine their surroundings. The train station appeared to be closed without a single light showing on the platform. Behind it, rolling hills disappeared into the distance. On the other side of the platform they could make out the ghostly silhouette of a dark, abandoned town. There were no lights on anywhere and everything was covered with a thick layer of what really did look like snow.

"Creepy." Marco said quietly, sniffling.

"And not good at all," said Nick, nodding. "It's worse than I thought. Nobody's been down here in a long time."

"Are you sure this is the right guy?"

Nick thought for a second before replying.

"What do we have on him?"

Marco, still sniffling, pulled out his tablet, flicked it on and started entering a query when they both heard footsteps in the distance. Marco quickly shut off the tablet, dousing the light. He looked to Nick, who gestured for Marco to follow him. Together, they made their way to the station building. The door was open. They went in and took up a position under the window, from where they could see while remaining hidden.

"I thought you said the coast was clear?" Nick whispered.

"He's supposed to be at work."

Marco flicked on the tablet and began furiously entering queries, his fingers moving faster and faster until they became a blur. A moment later he seemed to become disoriented, his typing slowed and he appeared to be dizzy.

"What's going on?" asked Nick.

"Hmm, must be the dust," Marco replied as he tried to refocus on the screen. "He's supposed to be at work..."

His voice trailed off. He looked as if he might collapse, but then regained his composure.

"Something... must have brought him..."

His eyes began to glaze over.

"Nick... I..."

"I've got you," said Nick.

He grabbed Marco before he fell over and eased him down against the wall. Nick eased the tablet from Marco's hands, flicked it off and tucked it in his coat.

"We don't need this right now. We've got to get you back."

"Is... dust?" Marco slurred, before passing out.

"No," Nick sighed. "Sorry, Marco, but I think you've got it too."

Suddenly, all the lights in the room came on. A door creaked open and Nick heard the sound of approaching footsteps on the stairs.

Doc Christmas and The Magic of Trains

CHAPTER 2

Company's Coming

"I'm not going to argue with you," Doc said curtly into his cell phone.

He sighed as the solid wood door creaked closed behind him, blocking out the cool breeze that heralded an early winter.

"I was able to get away early and if you're really going to come for a visit, then I'm going to have to clean up and get things at least a bit organized around here."

Carefully putting his briefcase in its usual spot, he pulled off his hospital ID tag and hung it on a hook. From the picture on the tag, Dr. Archibald Stevens stared back at him with an easy smile, mocking his dismal mood. He looked down, lined his shoes up neatly with his toe, then turned to look around as he listened to his daughter Vicki. Polished wood mouldings gleamed against a mix of old plaster walls and somewhat more recently rediscovered brick surfaces.

There wasn't a speck of dirt in sight. His house was as spotless and immaculate as it always was. During his visual inspection, Vicki continued.

"I appreciate it, Dad, I really do. It's been a while since she's seen you and we both miss you. Besides, this will be perfect for my project."

"Project? What does that mean?"

"It's not a big deal, I'll explain tomorrow. But, uh, Dad, there is one thing?"

"Go on," Doc asked, although he had a pretty good idea what was coming.

"Well, Jeanette talks about your trains all the time. She's completely enamored with them and hasn't seen them in so long. I know you said you hadn't touched them in a while, but could you make sure there's at least something for her to see? Maybe even a train to run?"

And there it was. Family was important, of course, but they weren't even here yet and already old wounds were being opened. Doc wrestled with that for a moment, pacing as he considered what should be a simple request, until he found himself standing in front of a door that he hadn't gone through in a very long time. He stared at the handmade sign on the door that his wife had given him years ago.

Train Room.

"You still there?"

He jumped as Vicki startled him from his thoughts. In that same moment, Doc found he'd instinctively reached for the door handle.

"I'm here."

He shook his head, then sighed as he turned the handle and opened the door. He flicked on the lights and slowly descended the stairs. Once he had reached the bottom, he continued his conversation.

"Look, Vicki, I don't know if I can do this. It's been a while. It may not even run."

"I know, but Dad, it's for Jeanette. Well, and for me too!"

Doc stood at the foot of the stairs and looked across the miniature world that he'd created. Spread out before him and covering most of the basement of the house, train tracks passed through realistic miniature mountains, past tilled fields and over streams and rivers, connecting an assortment of towns and villages. The colors and textures of the different seasons were reflected in various areas around the layout, but the largest feature by far was a snow covered mountain range that appeared to go on forever as it disappeared into a wall mural.

"I was always your biggest train fan, Dad," Vicki added sweetly.

Doc thought for a moment before he answered her. A flood of memories surged through his thoughts. Hearing Vicki as a little girl playing. Seeing her grown up, going off to college and then happily introducing him to the boy who would be Jeanette's father. Comforting her when that same boy left her even before Jeanette was born. Questioning her strength to go it alone and then admiring her firm resolve to finish her education. All those feelings flashed through his mind in an instant and somehow, today, made it so much easier to give in than to fight.

"I'll see what I can do."

"Yay!" a young, enthusiastic voice cried over the phone. "Thank you Grandpa!"

"You're welcome," Doc replied.

"Never mind, "said Vicki. "She's gone off to pack. But thanks. You've made her day, and mine!"

"I'll see you tomorrow." Doc hung up and slid the phone into his pocket. He folded his arms and wondered what he'd just committed to? He walked slowly over to the main control panel, reached down to an ornate cabinet and gently slid out the top drawer. Inside, a velvet lining cradled a beautifully detailed steam locomotive. As he carefully pulled the drawer out further, a full train of passenger cars emerged. Doc bent down for a closer inspection, then noticed the thick layer of dust covering the layout.

"This will never do," he muttered to himself.

He pushed the drawer back in, took a deep breath and blew.

CHAPTER 3

Careful!

Inside the station, Nick placed his hand gently on Marco's forehead. Nick frowned as he felt the much-too-high temperature. He pulled out Marco's tablet, flicked it to Com mode and was immediately and cheerily greeted.

"Marco, how's it going down there?"

"Not so well, Cyril. Marco is under the weather."

Nick glanced over his shoulder in the direction of the station window. He saw Doc Stevens reach the bottom of the stairs and pause as he examined his layout.

"And the Doctor... is in!"

"Just a sec, Nick," said Cyril sounding concerned. "I'll get DJ and..."

"Never mind, "Nick interrupted him. "I've got to get Marco back, but there's nothing I can do here yet. Just be ready and we'll be back as soon as we can get away. He's going to need attention.

"Roger that, Nick. We'll be waiting."

Nick closed the connection and checked Marco again, but there really wasn't anything he could do for him right now. He sighed as he moved over to the doorway and cautiously peered out.

Through the open doorway of the station, he saw Doc Stevens end his phone call and walk over to the layout. As he watched Doc carefully pull open the cabinet drawer, Nick thought he saw a spark of something in Doc's eyes, but it quickly vanished.

"This will never do." Nick heard Doc mutter to himself, as he slid the drawer closed and blew at the layer of dust.

Nick crept back inside the station as the dust cloud just created, wafted towards the portion of the layout where he and Marco were hiding.

"We could be here a while," he said to himself. "Unless..."

He took another look outside then moved quickly over to Marco and roused him.

"C'mon, we've got to go!"

"Mmm?"

Marco could hardly speak, and he was certainly no help. Nick helped him to his feet then grunted and hoisted him over his shoulder in a fireman's carry. Nick then made his way to the door of the station and positioned himself so that he could see both Doc and the train car at the same time.

Doc had rummaged around a little and had found a can of compressed air in his array of tools. He tried out a blast of compressed air on a portion of the layout and startled himself, as it created an even bigger cloud of dust, and knocked over some stuff in the process.

"That was stupid," said Doc. "It really has been a while

since I've worked on this!"

Nick knew that the dust cloud wasn't going to give them full cover. He then saw Doc reaching for a hand vacuum, and there was no way he wanted to wait around for that!

"We're going!" he told Marco.

Nick ran through the billowing haze across the platform as fast as he could. With Marco still on his shoulders, he climbed into the very same dilapidated old train car that they had arrived on.

Fortunately, Doc didn't see Nick's desperate sprint as he was beginning the process of tackling the dust problem with his hand vacuum. A moment later, Doc did notice something out of the corner of his eye. A fading glow emanated from a part of his train layout that depicted a dis-used train station with an abandoned passenger car parked on the siding.

Recalling that there were no lights on that part of the layout, Doc shut off the vacuum and went over for a closer look. But there was nothing there to see, just a dusty old station.

Doc Christmas and The Magic of Trains

CHAPTER 4

At the Hub

If there were a Grand Central Station of all the Grand Central Railroad Stations on the planet, the Hub's giant control center would have been able to fit it inside quite nicely and still have lots of room to spare. The impressive stone structure had been added to over the years and was now a mix of stone, steel, and brickwork.

A massive glowing hologram of Earth occupied nearly the entire top of the central dome. Spidery metal walkways floated at different levels around the globe and connected with steel staircases to the main platform surrounding the base. That platform was covered with rows of sparsely manned consoles. Beneath it all, arrays of train tracks and boarding platforms radiated out in multiple directions.

An alarm bell sounded as warning lights began flashing on one car of a row of odd-looking train cars parked on the tracks just below the Hub. It looked like a passenger car, but had odd-looking slots cut through its roof and sides with levers sticking out through the slots. As the alarm faded away, motors actuated and the levers began to move. Inside, the seats and walls that were attached to the levers moved with them, reconfiguring the car's interior.

Cyril, a bespectacled and wizened old elf, sat at the main console. He looked up from a monitor that showed the merging schematics of two train car interiors, and double-checked the location of a single flashing blue dot high on the hologram above.

His silvery earpieces crackled with a curt query.

"Is that them?"

He turned to the white-coated elf standing beside him.

"I'm right here, you know."

Doctor Jay, the head physician at the North Pole grinned at his success in even slightly ruffling Cyril's cool composure. His grin faded when Cyril smugly responded using only his initials.

"Hmm. Yes, 'DJ', it's them. Platform 1."

After a quick glare at Cyril for shortening his name, DJ nodded to his medical team then followed them down toward the reconfigured and now glowing train car. As soon as the glow began to diminish, the team hopped aboard. They emerged moments later carrying the unconscious Marco whom they carefully laid on a waiting gurney.

DJ examined him quickly then glanced up at Nick as he stepped down from the train.

"What happened? I thought he was okay?"

"He was fine when we left," Nick confirmed sadly. "It seems like the trip sped the process up. He got woozy really fast, collapsed and then just passed out."

"Nothing else?"

"It was dusty."

"Well, that wouldn't do anything," said DJ as he shook his head. "I'll let you know, but, he seems just like the rest."

"So it's still spreading?" asked Nick.

"I've nothing new to tell you," DJ replied sadly. "I was hoping that you'd have some good news for me?"

Now it was Nick's turn to shake his head. DJ simply nodded and with a sigh, turned to follow his team as they rolled Marco away.

Cyril had come down from his console.

"He's right Nick. Nothing new here. How did you do?"

"Not good," said Nick. 'We can't just go to him. There's no way he'll be able to help us in his current state of mind."

"Okay. So? You have a plan?"

Nick looked at Cyril grimly.

"I think we'll have to bring him here. As is. And hope for the best."

"What? Is that even possible?" asked Cyril.

"Tell Fetna to get things ready up above," Nick was focusing now. "I'll need a good cover story. Something that will get me right inside. He was on the phone to his daughter about a visit. Maybe we can use that?"

Nick walked away as Fetna rappelled down onto the platform from the upper levels of the dome. As Cyril briefed him on what had just transpired, Fetna's expression altered between sad and serious, until Cyril mentioned bringing Doc to the pole.

Fetna grinned. He released a catch on the bungee-like cord on which he had arrived and launched himself back up into the rafters.

"I'll get the landing ready," said Fetna, his slivery ear-pieces glinting in the holographic Earthlight as he ascended.

15

CHAPTER 5

Catching Up

A knock on the richly paneled door preceded Helga's entry. The stoic German had been Doc's family housekeeper for over 10 years and had stayed on after his wife passed away. When she entered his study without waiting for a response, Doc knew it was for something unusual.

"They're here?" he guessed.

"Yes, Doctor Stevens," Helga replied, seeming even more rigid than usual. "They just pulled up."

Doc knew that this meant that she'd been watching, which also meant that she was probably worried.

"They will only be here for a few days, Helga."

She said nothing so he continued.

"I really appreciate the extra help while they are here. I don't think I could handle them alone."

"They are your family, Doctor. You don't need my help."

Confused by her response, Doc tried again.

"Well, I mean with the meals then, I do appreciate your help. Can you please greet them? I'll be right there."

Helga nodded and left the study. When she acted like this Doc almost expected that she'd click her heels.

He steeled himself to meet his daughter. It had been a long time and he knew that his now customary, albeit solitary, ways were about to be tested by the trials of having family around. He just wanted to get through it so that things could return to normal.

He made a mental note of the page number and closed the book he'd been reading. He stood up and took a glance around his paneled study. Everything seemed reassuringly in order. The only things missing were the pictures he'd taken down. There had been too many memories hanging in the room and he'd been unable to relax or think in the study. Consequently he'd done what he considered to be the right thing and had removed the pictures so he could get back to work. Satisfied once again about that decision, he headed out of the study.

Helga had just greeted Vicki and Jeanette when he reached the hallway. Jeanette spotted him first.

"Grandpa!" she yelled.

She skirted around Helga and her disapproving stare, dashed down the hall and jumped up for a hug, almost knocking Doc over in the process.

"Jeanette!" Vicki exclaimed, half-heartedly.

"It's quite alright," said Doc, trying to avoid hugging back. "No harm done."

He gave Jeanette the briefest of squeezes then let go. He extended his hand to Vicki, who brushed it aside and gave him a big hug.

"You *are* out of practice," she said jokingly as she let him go. "But it's good to see you."

"And the trains!" added Jeanette, excitedly.

"Yes, and the trains," Vicki agreed, as she looked inquisitively at Doc.

"Hmm," said Doc, trying to sound noncommittal. "Well, I was able to get some things sorted out, so you will be able to run a train."

"Yay!" Jeanette exclaimed, before she whirled and headed for the train room.

"You'd better go see what she's up to," Helga said to Vicki. "Dinner will be ready in about an hour."

"Dinner?" Vicki asked.

"Helga will be helping out while you're visiting," said Doc. "I don't cook much any more and Helga has, er, offered."

He still wasn't sure why Helga had snapped at him earlier and he didn't want to upset her. However she seemed fine with his explanation and almost gave Vicki a smile as she walked away.

* * *

Doc had indeed spent some time in the train room. The layout was clean and dust free, although a few things were slightly jumbled from the cleaning process. Vicki looked things over then started straightening a few things out for him, pointedly letting him deal with Jeanette. He helped Jeanette choose a diesel locomotive and some freight cars. She had them all set up on the track before he could even ask if she needed help.

When he thought they all were done setting up, she looked up to him.

"Where's the caboose Grandpa?" she asked.

"Trains today don't usually have cabooses."

"Well, I'd like to have a caboose on this train."

19

Doc took a caboose from the car box and Jeanette carefully added it to her train.

Doc then powered up the control panel and flicked some switches that lit up the layout. Lights in buildings came on, a Ferris wheel began spinning, and cars and trucks started driving along the model roadway. The miniature world came to life, as did a huge sparkle in Jeanette's eyes. Vicki went to stand beside them at the control panel.

"Wow, Grandpa. It's so great!" Jeanette whispered.

"It is great, Dad." Vicki added. "Thanks for setting it up."

"Can I run the train now?" asked Jeanette.

Doc showed her how the panels on the controls matched the tracks on the layout and where the train would go. He handed her a controller and prepared to give her a talk on how to run the trains.

"Now, these are not toy trains, Jeanette, so..."

"Grandpa!" Jeanette interrupted. "I'm eight now. I remember what to do. You told me before when I was little. 'These are not toys but models and you have to drive them kinda slow and not too crazy, so they look like real trains if you were *this small*'. Don't you remember?"

She held up two fingers and squinted at him through the gap between them.

"I told you she remembered your trains," Vicki laughed, smiling at her daughter.

"Go on, take it out then," said Doc, gesturing at the train.

Jeanette turned the knob and eased the train out the yard and around the layout, walking along with the wireless remote so that she could see the train going around the layout as if she was 'this small'.

Doc and Vicki watched while the train made a couple of trips around the layout, then, just as Doc was going to excuse himself and go upstairs, Vicki forestalled him. "I need to go unpack and get us settled in. Would you mind watching her? She's going to be really tired after the long drive and all this train excitement and I want to be ready for that."

Doc had no choice but to agree. Fortunately, Jeanette seemed quite content to leave him to his own devices. She ran the train, occasionally asking to change a car or switch tracks while he cleaned tracks and continued straightening things up.

Before too long dinner was ready.

* * *

Vicki had been wise to get prepared. Jeanette barely made it through dinner. Vicki thought that she was asleep as she carried Jeanette upstairs. However when she laid her down on the bed, Jeanette asked a really tough question.

"What's wrong with Grandpa?" she said, half asleep. "He seems kinda sad."

"He is sad. He's sad about Grandma Marilee."

"Do you think Grandpa will still put up a Christmas tree like Grandma Marilee used to?"

"I don't know sweetie, but lets not ask him just yet. If he's planning to, it might spoil the surprise!"

"Mmm, okay," said Jeanette, before falling asleep.

Vicki slid up Jeanette's covers, eased her door shut and headed down to the main floor. Doc was just saying goodbye to Helga and thanking her again for putting in the extra time.

"Thank You!" Vicki called to Helga as the door closed behind her. "She seems the same as I remember."

"What do you mean?" said Doc, defensively.

"Nothing, Dad, She seems nice."

"I don't know," said Doc. "She seemed a bit off today."

"You're lucky to have her here. She's a good friend."

"She's not a friend. She's a housekeeper."

He could tell that Vicki wasn't going to let the matter drop, so he changed the subject.

"Would you like a glass of sherry?"

"I don't drink sherry. Have you got red wine?"

He thought he didn't, but after searching for a few minutes, located a bottle in the last place he looked, in his formerly empty wine cellar.

"I don't remember buying all that wine," he said, as he uncorked the bottle.

Vicki smiled. "Like I said Dad, it seems like Helga is a good friend."

He simply glared at her, ignored her comment and then changed the subject.

"Is Jeanette okay upstairs?"

"Definitely. She's already asleep."

"Hmm. Well she seems pretty smart, like her mother".

"Thanks, Dad, but too smart I think, sometimes."

"What do you mean?"

"Well," Vicki replied hesitantly. "She wanted to know why you're so sad."

"Don't start, Vicki," Doc sighed.

"Sorry, but it's hard for her. She remembers you the way you... used to be."

Doc thought for a moment.

"Things have changed," he said quietly.

"I know, Dad, but she doesn't understand."

He sighed and looked away.

"Okay, well I'm off to bed too then," said Vicki. "See you in the morning."

"Goodnight."

Doc turned back to his sherry. It was exactly the conversation he hadn't wanted to have. He took a final small sip of his sherry then headed off to bed himself.

CHAPTER 6

Off To Work

If there was one staple in Doc's life it had always been a nice hot cup of tea, sipped quietly first thing in the morning before breakfast. When he came down to find Jeanette loudly playing dance party in the sitting room and Vicki and Helga in the kitchen busily chatting away over coffee, he assumed that even morning tea would be another casualty of this visit. He was therefore pleasantly surprised when Helga got up and poured him a nice steaming cup of... coffee.

He sighed and thanked her graciously. After all, Helga wasn't usually there in the mornings and couldn't be blamed for not knowing.

The maelstrom around him began to subside as Vicki called Jeanette for breakfast and they all gathered at the table.

"We need one more place setting," said Vicki as she sat down.

"What?" Helga asked, in surprise. "For who?"

"For you of course."

Helga looked as if she was going to protest.

Vicki added. "If you're hanging about here to help just because of us," Vicki added. "then you can darn well join us."

Helga glanced at Doc, who nodded agreement, but it really didn't matter, since Vicki was already moving chairs to make room for her at the table.

* * *

When they were finally seated and starting to eat, Vicki, turned to Doc.

"Tell me again how you and Helga know each other?"

"Trains," he replied, quickly taking another bite to forestall further questioning.

Vicki looked at Helga.

"Trains?"

"Yes," said Helga. "My father was an engineer. Some of my best memories as a child were when my mother would take me down to the train line to see a train he was driving go by. One time, he was going very slowly and she ran alongside and handed me up to him."

She paused and looked pointedly at Jeanette.

"That was very dangerous but it was so wonderful at the time. Anyway, ever since, I have loved trains."

"Me too!" Jeanette exclaimed.

Helga ignored her and continued.

"I joined the Railroad Historical Association so I can be around steam trains just like my father used to drive. While there I met your father. He had lent his riding train to the association for an event. Eventually, he helped me find work and then offered me a part-time job as well."

"You never told me that story about your father," said Doc.

"You are a very busy man, Doctor Stevens," Helga replied politely.

"What's a riding train Grandpa?" asked Jeanette.

He rolled his eyes and looked away.

"It's just like it sounds honey," said Vicki. "It's another kind of model train that you can ride on. It's much bigger than the trains downstairs"

Jeanette opened her mouth and Doc knew the question that was coming, so he answered it for her.

"Sorry, but you can't go for a ride. I lent it to the train club for their Christmas display and it's already down there."

"At the Mall?" Vicki asked him.

He nodded.

"But I don't go down there. They run it just fine without me."

Jeanette looked like she might cry at such a harsh answer, but Vicki countered that easily.

"Well, honey, we'll get over there sometime so you can ride on Grandpa's train at the mall too."

All this train talk was making Doc crazy. He decided he'd have to change the subject.

"Vicki, you mentioned something about your school. How's that going?"

"She's finished!" Jeanette answered proudly, on her mom's behalf.

"I'm finished classes," Vicki corrected her. "I still have my final assignment to do and then on to practicum."

"And this thing you mentioned yesterday, about this trip being good for it. What's that about?" asked Doc.

"Yes, Dad. Well, I was thinking..."

Doc's phone rang. He checked the display and it was the hospital.

"Excuse me," he said to Vicki before answering the call. "Hello... Yes, well that sounds very good... I'll be in soon... Thanks."

He hung up and looked at Vicki, who seemed ready to pick up right where she left off.

"Sorry, but it seems I have to go in to work," he apologized.

Undaunted and without skipping a beat, Vicki surprised him.

"That's great. Mind if I tag along?"

"What about Jeanette?"

"I'll stay here with Helga," said Jeanette.

"Sorry child, but I have to clean up."

"That's okay, I can help. And we can talk about real steam engines!"

Jeanette was clearly in awe of this woman who hung out with real trains.

"That's not..." Doc began.

"No, I don't think that will work," said Helga.

Vicki quickly came to Jeanette's defense.

"Helga, she's a really good cleaner-upper, and I'm sure she won't bother you too much about trains."

Helga sniffed.

"I'd really appreciate some time with my dad," Vicki said sweetly.

Finally coerced, Helga agreed in her own way.

"If you must."

"Thank you, Helga." Jeanette said very quietly.

Doc stared open-mouthed. He'd just been completely outmaneuvered!

CHAPTER 7

A Triumph

Doc felt like a total schmuck by the time they pulled into the hospital parking lot. Vicki had tried to talk about the fall colors in the trees with him a couple of times, but he'd just stonewalled her. It wasn't a long trip but it seemed to him that he'd somehow earned the right to sit in uncomfortable silence for the rest of the drive. He wasn't sure whether it bothered him more that Vicki was giving him space or that he felt so bad about why. He was her father, after all.

"Dad! What's that?" Vicki suddenly blurted out.

Looking around quickly, Doc had no idea what she was talking about.

"What?"

"That."

She pointed out the window at a sign on the wall of the

hospital. '*Stevens Wing. Infectious Disease Research Laboratory*'.

"Oh, that."

She looked at him, puzzled.

He sighed.

"At you mother's request, I donated some money to the hospital in her name after she passed. They figured that it had to be named after her, so..."

He gestured at the wall. What he didn't explain to Vicki is how he'd fought them hard so that the sign didn't say 'Marilee Stevens Wing'. He couldn't have come to work each day if he'd had to endure the pain of being reminded that she was gone, day in and day out. It was hard enough as it was.

"Dad," said Vicki, almost sobbing. "That's so great."

He gave her a half smile as he swung the car into his parking stall, where there was a sign that read '*RESERVED - Department Head*'.

"Yes, they made me head of the department as well."

He could feel her gaze as she took in this new information.

"Why didn't you tell me?"

"It didn't seem important, and frankly since then I've been too busy to think about it."

That part was true. He'd kept himself more than busy since then. He shut of the car's engine.

"Come inside and meet Tommy."

* * *

Tommy was just like any other normal kid. The only thing odd was the fact he was being quarantined in a sealed chamber and that to examine him, Doc had to don a full isolation suit. Tommy's tests had come back as negative, so while he could have probably been given the all clear over the phone, Doc wanted to make sure for himself. He double-checked the test results outside and then donned his protective gear and went in to see Tommy in person.

Inside the isolation chamber he checked the last few charts and indicators. They too pronounced that Tommy was all clear.

"Am I going to be okay, Dr. Stevens?" asked Tommy.

For all that he'd been through this was one polite 11 year old.

"You sure are, Tommy!"

Doc pulled off his headpiece and smiled, unsealing the shroud positioned around Tommy. He motioned to Tommy's parents waiting in the viewing hall that it was okay to enter.

Before they arrived Doc whispered to Tommy.

"Maybe next time your dad takes you to South America, don't play in the dirt and definitely don't play with the bugs."

He winked at Tommy and then turned to fend off a seemingly unending stream of heartfelt handshakes, thanks, and assorted blessings from Tommy's dad, along with sobbing and hugs from his mother.

After several failed attempts to leave, Doc finally broke free and joined Vicki in the hallway.

"Another miracle!" she said, smiling at him.

"Just good science at work." He replied, with a shrug, looking back at Tommy and his parents. "I'm glad he pulled through."

"So, what was wrong with him? With the isolation chamber and everything?"

He looked at her carefully.

"You really want to know?"

"I really do."

"Okay. He caught a fairly contagious virus while he was visiting his dad in South America. Then he was bitten by a poisonous beetle. Somehow the two things combined then attacked his immune system."

"That sounds awful!"

"It nearly was. They stabilized him, but the virus mutated and became something else entirely.

They contacted me and I was able to figure it out with some help from Dr. O'Brien at the Tate Institute in Ireland. Once we knew what we had, we came up with a vaccine that worked on everyone."

Vicki was puzzled.

"Everyone?"

Doc looked at her grimly.

"Everyone that came into contact with Tommy got sick. He was a real patient zero. Anyway, once we had the vaccine I had Tommy moved here so I could work on him. Today is the first day that I can guarantee that he's both virus free and no longer contagious."

"Amazing!"

"Not really. Just doing my job,"

For a moment Doc was almost embarrassed at how much he'd told her.

"I'd better get back to the lab."

"What, no celebration?" said Vicki. "You did great. You should take a minute and enjoy."

"I really should get back."

Vicki was having none of that.

"I'm taking you for lunch. Besides, we have things to talk about."

CHAPTER 8

Proud of You Dad

At the restaurant Doc knew there was more happening than just a celebratory meal.

"So why are you taking me for lunch, really? You mentioned something on the phone and again at breakfast. So what do you want from me?"

"Well," Vicki began, "I have to do a final project to get my Journalism degree, and I want to do the project on you. An article on your career, like a mini-biography."

He could see where this would lead. Vicki and Jeanette would be around for weeks or even months while Vicki put her paper together. His life would be completely disrupted.

"I don't think that's a good idea," said Doc shaking his head.

"Look, Dad, like it or not you're a bit of a hero. From the time you saved that lady at the train station right up until today. Just ask Tommy's parents."

Doc was still shaking his head.

"It's just about your work, nothing personal."

"No," said Doc, firmly.

"Fine," Vicki said, sharply.

They sat in silence for a few minutes until the waitress came over and topped up their coffees. They both thanked her at the exactly same time then looked at each other.

"Jinx," Vicki said, without smiling.

Doc finally smiled and Vicki smiled back at him.

"So, how did you find Tommy's cure?"

"Is this for your article?" Doc asked.

"Possibly. Dad, I love what you do. I just can't figure out how you do it when nobody else can."

"That's not fair," said Doc. "I couldn't do what I do *without* everyone else's help. If Franz Heightman hadn't published that paper on rare beetle stings in South America, I wouldn't have known where to begin to look."

"Yes, but weren't you the one who convinced him and a bunch of these specialists to share their work, rather than hoard it in the hope of fame and fortune?"

"I suppose. It seems stupid for us to work independently on the same thing, so now we focus and share."

"And what's been happening since then?"

"Well, things like Tommy getting cured do seem to happen more often."

"Exactly," Vicki pointed out. "But you came up with the antidote this time, and usually do."

Doc thought for a moment before replying.

"I'm a hands on guy, Vicki, I just can't separate the science from the people it's affecting. Too many people want to hand off everything that's not easy or convenient and want to specialize. Specialization is great, but someone has to pull it all together."

He almost laughed.

"Listen to me lecturing!"

"I like to listen to you talk, Dad. You have a different viewpoint than most. Actually, I'm not quite sure how to convey that to people in your biography."

Doc's phone rang.

"Go ahead," said Vicki.

Thinking it was the hospital again, Doc answered without looking at the call display.

"Hello".

"Hi Doc," said a familiar voice. "This is Roger from Eastside Hobbies."

"Oh. Hi Roger."

"I know we haven't talked for a while, but there's this reporter fellow here in the store. He's only in town for a couple of days and looking to do a story on a 'Christmassy' layout."

"Okay?" Doc replied cautiously, as Vicki watched him curiously.

"Well, you're the only one I know around here that has a good Christmas scene on his layout," Roger continued. "And, well, would you like to show it to him?"

"I don't think so," replied Doc. "It's not really... ready."

"That's kinda what I thought," Roger said, before he was interrupted by the sound of his store's entry bell. "Excuse me for a minute?"

Doc covered the phone as he waited.

"Some reporter wants to do a story on my layout," he said to Vicki.

"Well, why not..." Vicki started to ask.

"Hello?" said a new voice from the other end of the phone.

"Hello?" Doc replied.

"Hi, My name is Nick Field. I'm the reporter that Roger was just talking about. Look, it seems he's a bit busy now and I have a deadline tomorrow. Is there any way I could come by and talk to you about your layout? Roger says it's the best one around and I need a cute Christmassy bit for the Sunday section of *The Northern Times*."

Doc glanced at Vicki who was looking questioningly at him. He loved her but really wished that she'd find a project other than him to work on. That gave him an idea. He gave her a brief smile

"Sure," he said to Nick. "I guess if Roger said that. How's tomorrow afternoon around four?"

"Great," said Nick , then added. "But, er, is there any way we can do it today? My deadline is tomorrow, but I still have to write it all up and get a few pictures."

Doc smiled to himself.

"Oh I see. Okay, well, four o'clock at the house today then. We're at 16 Ventura Lane."

"That's great, thanks," said Nick, happily. "See you at four."

"You're welcome, see you then."

Doc hung up and smiled at Vicki.

"Well?" she asked.

"I guess Roger at the hobby shop recommended my train layout to some journalist from *The Northern Times*. He's looking to do a story on a train layout with a Christmas theme. I hope you don't mind."

"Why would I mind?"

"Well, since you and Jeanette are, uh, so happy about the trains running, maybe you can help me give this fellow a tour."

"Of course. It'll be lovely to have a real journalist to talk to. I'm sure Jeanette's going to be thrilled too!"

"Good, he's coming over at four o'clock. I'll count on your help."

"I'm glad you're finally showing your layout again," said Vicki smiling.

CHAPTER 9

The Reporter

At precisely four o'clock, the heavy front door of Doc's house swung open to reveal a friendly-looking fellow of indeterminate age, dressed business-casual with a light overcoat and sporting a trim grey-black beard. An easy confident smile accompanied his words.

"You must be Doctor Stevens."

Doc nodded as Vicki joined him at the door.

"My name's Nick. Nick Field."

Vicki chimed in before Doc could answer.

"I'm his daughter, Vicki. Welcome Mr. Field."

"Yes, please come in," Doc added.

"Thanks, and please, call me Nick," he said, stepping through the doorway. "I prefer it, especially when I'm working afield."

Doc ignored the joke, but Vicki smiled in appreciation.

As Vicki hung Nick's coat up, Jeanette came down the stairs. She walked right up behind Nick and as he turned, she introduced herself.

"I'm Jeanette."

"Pleased to meet you, Miss Jeanette. I'm Nick. Will you be joining us on our tour today?"

Jeanette shrugged and looked at her mother. Vicki nodded.

"This is my daughter."

"We're showing Nick the train layout today Jeanette," Doc explained. "Would you like to be our guide?"

"Uh-huh!"

She nodded and spun around then marched over to the train room door. Turning briefly to make sure that everyone was following, she opened the door and headed downstairs.

"Right this way."

* * *

Doc knew that his layout could seem impressive, although there were things about it that would definitely make devout model railroaders cringe. He'd laid it out in seasons, from winter through spring, and the layout occupied the entire length of the basement. Hand painted backdrops blended with the scenery adding further realism to the miniature world. Trains could take multiple routes to connect the various towns and cities across the imaginary lands. And everything was complete down to the last detail. All except for one area.

When Marilee had passed away, he'd simply stopped working on the layout at the end depicting spring and that area hadn't been touched since. For some reason, that uncompleted section was where Jeanette decided to start her tour. Vicki was perplexed too.

"Why are we starting here, honey?"

"This is where you can see all the things that make it work before it looks like that."

Jeanette pointed at the framed artwork on the wall behind them. Memories flooded Doc's mind as they all walked over and studied Marilee's hand-drawn depiction of the completed layout. Damn it, Doc thought. This was exactly why he didn't come down here any more.

Fortunately, Vicki noticed the pained expression on Doc's face.

"When dad started talking about building a layout,"she explained, "we all sat down and each made lists of all the things that we wanted to have on the layout."

"Interesting," said Nick.

"Dad made a plan detailing how he thought the tracks, towns, and terrain should look. My mom drew it up and colored it in. Dad's been building towards it ever since."

"Except for one thing," Jeanette added.

"What's that?" Nick asked.

"They forgot the street car," replied Jeanette seriously.

"Oh, I see," said Nick.

"It seems there were a few details that someone else thought would be nice," Vicki explained.

Nick looked at them all and then turned to face the layout's incomplete section. An oval of track in the new section didn't seem to connect to any of the other tracks. He looked at Jeanette and pointed at the oval.

"It looks like maybe this is where it should go?"

"Yes!" she exclaimed. "That's it exactly!"

"Hmmm, and maybe a town here?" said Nick. "That the streetcar goes through?"

Jeanette nodded, then turned to her mother.

"I told you!"

"Yes you did," said Vicki. "Now, can we continue the tour?"

"I think that's a good idea," Doc agreed, ever more eager get this over with. "Lets start here at the spring end and work our way over to winter. Vicki, would you like to do the honors?"

"Is that okay, honey?" she asked Jeanette.

"Sure, " replied Jeanette, before turning to Doc. "Can we get some trains for each section, Grandpa?"

He nodded and they went to collect some trains while Vicki commenced the tour.

CHAPTER 10

Doc's Layout

"So this unfinished section is going to represent a 1950's town, sort of '*Anywhere in North America*'," Vicki explained. There will be a diner, a drive in theater, a small bustling town center, and yes, a streetcar connecting it all together. Everyday life here will revolve around the train station at the center of town. In the industrial area, trains will deliver cargo in boxcars to the freight depot and carloads of wood to the lumberyard on the outskirts of town."

While Nick took some time to look around under the bench work, Doc and Jeanette had found the logging train and were busy setting it up to run in the next area of the layout.

Vicki approached them and really started to get into her narrator role.

"Lumber for the town's lumberyard will come from the hills high above the town," she said gesturing at the ridge just beyond the town. "In the 1930's after trees were felled they were dragged by steam tractor to the rail line."

Vicki pointed out the loggers and the model steam tractor while Jeanette slowly ran a small black logging engine with a few cars loaded with logs down from the tree line.

"Trees are then moved by the logging railroad through the camp and down to the sawmill adjacent to the main line."

"This is so very well done!" Nick said as he watched the logs arrive at the mill.

"Ready!" Doc called out.

Vicki took Nick around to the other side of the model ridge.

"Over here it's summer in the late 1800's. When the railroads were first built, they logged out one tree at a time and horses pulled the logs to a small mill, where they were cut into railroad ties, loaded on flat cars, and sent on to the railhead."

Jeanette pushed a button on her controller. The long drawn out wail of a steam whistle announced the wood burning engine's arrival with a fresh load of ties.

"At the railhead and working mostly by hand, crews cleared the land, dropped ties and spiked down rails to push the line forward across the prairies. A sparse and rowdy tent camp travelled along near the rails' end, always moving along with the construction. Conditions at the railhead were harsh and the mobile town earned the nickname '*Hell on Wheels*'. However, no matter what happened there, the line crawled inexorably westward."

Vicki pointed forward to the next range of model hills.

"What does index-horribly mean?" asked Jeanette.

"Well, honey," Vicki hesitated, not prepared for the question. "It means..."

"It means that it just keeps going. Nothing can stop it," said Doc. "It just keeps going."

Vicki indicated the bright foliage on some of the trees in the next area.

"In these mountains, summer is drawing to a close, but that isn't stopping the coal mining work. And of course after wood burning engines came?"

"Coal!" Jeanette exclaimed.

"That's right," said Vicki. "Coal-fired steam engines. Coal had been mined for smelting steel and warming homes but it also created a hotter fire and a more efficient steam engine until..."

"Diesel!" yelled Jeanette.

Right on cue, a train presided over by a small diesel-powered mining engine drove along the track. It came out of the mineshaft and over to the coal tipple where it's black cargo was sent tumbling down to the piles below, awaiting later transfer to hopper cars on the main line.

Vicki nodded.

"The development of the diesel engine was a death knell for steam engines. Well, that and the acceptance of the automobile. With the independence that cars provided, passenger train travel was nearly eliminated."

She pointed to an abandoned town and train station just off the main line. One that Nick was very familiar with.

"Towns whose existence depended on coal mines and trains were the hardest hit, and many vanished or became ghost towns."

"You know Vicki," said Nick, "you could do this for a living. You definitely have a way with words."

"I'm actually just finishing my Journalism degree," she said, glancing over at Doc. "Just one final project to do."

Doc shook his head before Jeanette got things moving again.

"Mom!"

Just ahead, a big split in the layout's bench work had been made to look like a riverbank on each side. On the side they'd just left, the rails snaked away from the coal mine and past a few other towns and villages before crossing a trestle over a deep gorge and dipping into a tunnel. Vicki ignored all that and went to the other side of the river. She noticed Nick looking at the sections she'd passed over.

"There are so many little areas to see that we could be here for weeks," She explained.

She pointed at a hillside with little bumps in the grassy meadow.

"Those are rabbits!"

Nick put on his glasses as she handed him her phone. She showed him how to use the camera to magnify the size of rabbits.

"That's amazing," he said.

"There is special stuff everywhere!" Jeanette added.

"Grandpa used to play a game where he'd hide a plastic person on the layout and I'd have to find him! What was his name?"

Doc hadn't thought about that in years.

"Bob," he said slowly. "His name's Bob."

"'*Where's Bob?*' That was the game!" Jeanette smiled. "Where is he, Grandpa?"

Before Doc could answer, and before Jeanette became fixated on finding Bob, Vicki spoke up.

"We have a lot more to show Nick, Jeanette."

She looked sad.

"And we can certainly look for Bob during the rest of the tour," Nick added, looking directly at Doc.

Doc was confused and was't sure what he meant. Vicki hadn't noticed and continued the tour.

"Here we have a departure from tradition. On this side

of the water, we've moved over to England."

The main line emerged from a tunnel into what resembled the English countryside in fall. It snaked along a river, and passed through a station in a distinctively English town.

"Why the change in country?" asked Nick.

Vicki looked at Doc, but he ignored her. He'd decided that this was her show and she could run it.

"It was either because a certain little girl was once a fan of Thomas the Tank Engine or because it just seemed the right thing to do."

She seemed to be expecting Doc to add something, but he remained silent.

"This entire peninsula is modeled after railways in England. The old English architecture is quite distinctive and beautiful, as are British trains. There's even a funicular cliff railway that ferries passengers from the lower town to the upper town where residents can have tea and enjoy an uninterrupted view of the port. Dad spent quite a lot of time on that."

"I had to!" Doc protested. "They don't make model ships in the proper size."

Around the tip of the peninsula, cargo ships loaded and unloaded goods from trains and trucks.

"I like this part," said Jeanette, pulling Nick over to the next section.

On the other side of the estuary, time and space shifted again. A huge container port had a modern city as a backdrop.

"And why's that?" Nick asked.

"I get to drive trains faster here!" whispered Jeanette.

She cranked the throttle on the remote that Doc had just handed her and a sleek bullet train whispered out of the station, through the city, and into the rolling hills beyond.

"Not too fast, Jeanette," Vicki cautioned, before explaining things further to Nick. "This modern city is a combination of cultures and transportation models. All over the world countries are seeing a huge resurgence of passenger rail travel. Here we have light rail transit, a monorail, and even a subway."

Sure enough, a cutaway in the benchwork showed an underground station. As they watched a subway train pulled in and stopped, waiting for passengers to get on and off, then started up and headed out of the station.

"Incredible," said Nick, as he looked around the city. He pointed out a couple of vehicles that were moving down the roadway by themselves. "How are these cars and busses moving?"

"Magic," said Jeanette.

"Actually, by magnets," Vicki clarified, as the bus pulled up to red light and stopped. "These are special vehicles and roadways. They even stop and go at traffic lights!"

"Magic," Jeanette repeated.

Nick smiled at her.

'Anyway," said Vicki. "Now we can finish fall and get into the winter area... and the part of the layout that you most came to see?"

"That's right. It is a holiday piece," Nick added smiling.

"Well, as you can see, behind the city the terrain gets much higher. The train also goes through forests and small towns that were likely great vacation spots during the summer."

Nick's phone rang, startling them all.

"Sorry," he said, pulling his phone from his pocket. "Excuse me. Hello?"

He listened for a minute before replying carefully.

"Are you sure?"

Doc recognized the 'really-bad-news-but-I-won't-let-on' expression that crossed Nick's face. He'd seen that look on people's faces before.

"Okay, I'll see what I can do," said Nick, before ending the call.

"Everything alright?" Doc asked.

"Dad!"

"It's okay, Vicki." said Nick, turning to Doc. "You're very intuitive. I do have to run off and deal with something."

"What?" said Doc bluntly, as Vicki glared at him.

"Just a small problem up North. Nothing to worry about," Nick explained as he smiled reassuringly. "I do need to get back to my hotel and see if I can do anything from there. Otherwise I may have to head back home. If I'm still here, would it be alright if I call you tomorrow and try and come by to finish the tour and maybe get some pictures?"

"Yes," Doc replied grudgingly.

The tone of his voice earned him another glare from Vicki and a disturbingly similar look from Jeanette. Nick either didn't notice or didn't care and they all headed back upstairs. At the top of the stairs, Nick paused and looked back at the snowy Christmas section of the layout with an odd look in his eyes.

"It's a wonderful layout you've built," Nick told Doc as he looked back from the doorway. "Full of Magic! You must show it often?"

Doc sighed.

"You are the first person I've shown it to in years, other than Vicky, plus Roger and a couple of others from the club."

"Well' it's a shame more people can't see it. It's truly marvelous. Listen, I'm going to put my notes together this evening. If I can stay in town, I'd like to get some background on the man behind the layout and maybe a few pictures?"

Doc opened his mouth to say no, but closed it when he received a preemptive disapproving look from both Vicki and Jeanette.

"Of course," said Vicki, easing her dad aside. "Do you have a ride to your hotel?"

"No, I was just going to grab a cab."

"Nonsense," said Vicki. "I'll drop you."

"Thank you, Vicki, that would be helpful. Doctor Stevens."

He bid Doc goodbye and Doc nodded back.

"Miss Jeanette," said Nick.

"Bye." Jeanette replied looking slightly sad.

Nick gave Jeanette a wink as the door closed between them.

* * *

"I'm really sorry about my dad," said Vicki as soon as she and Nick were in the car.

"Sorry?" said Nick, in surprise. "Why?"

"He's just not himself. He hasn't been for years, ever since mom died."

"He's hurting, that's plain to see. But he has you and Jeanette."

"Well, we're only here for a visit." Vicki said, sadly. "First one in two years!"

Nick looked at her with a reassuring smile.

"Don't be too hard on him. I'm sure he'll come around."

They discussed some of the finer details of Doc's layout for a few minutes.

"Here's my hotel, "said Nick. "Thanks for the ride."

"You're very welcome," said Vicki, as Nick got out of the car.

Vicki smiled and waved as she watched Nick walk into the hotel.

CHAPTER 11

He Has To Go

As he entered the hotel lobby, Nick smiled at the woman behind the front desk. All the other desk staff were working, along with a couple of other employees, on a few tables that had been set up in the front lobby. An artificial Christmas tree was up but not yet decorated and the rest of the tables had been set up around the tree in a pattern that Nick found quite familiar. Still, he decided he'd better check.

"Hello, Anika," he asked, recognizing one of the people working there.

The concierge smiled up at him.

"Oh, hello, Mr. Field. What can we do for you?"

"Nothing really. I was just curious. What are you up to here?"

"Well, we set up a holiday display each year with a Christmas tree, a train and presents, You know. Holiday things to help guests feel at home if they are staying here during the holidays."

Nick smiled.

"That's a great idea. And it's working, too. I feel more at home already just knowing it'll be here!"

"We'll have the main parts setup soon, then we ask guests if they'd like to help decorate. Will you be able to join us sometime?" Anika asked, politely.

"I most certainly will, "Nick replied. "If I am still in town."

"Will you be leaving us soon?"

"I'm not sure yet," said Nick. "I have an important project that needs completing as soon as possible."

Anika smiled again and nodded.

"Well you're always welcome."

"Thank you Anika," said Nick, then headed to the elevator.

* * *

He stepped out of the elevator and headed for his room. Really he didn't need a room, but it was handy to have a place to leave things. Nick made sure the 'Do Not Disturb' sign was still out and then he opened the door. It was an ordinary enough hotel room, but there was no sign that anyone had been inside since the room had been cleaned. His odd-looking briefcase and a day bag were sitting on the bed, the only items that didn't come with the room.

Nick reached into his day bag and slid out an elfPad. When he flicked it on he was instantly connected with Cyril.

"Hi Nick."

Cyril looked worried and there was an unusual timbre in his voice.

"Cyril. No improvement?"

"Actually things are worse."

Nick grimaced.

"Show me," he said, setting the elfPad face up on the bed.

A brighter light sprang from the tablet's surface as it entered 3D mode. Directly above the tablet a row of holographically projected monitors echoed what Cyril was seeing on his screens. Even Cyril's image had moved to one of the projected monitors, his elven earpieces flashing.

"It's still spreading. Isolating the unaffected has also proven ineffective."

One monitor flickered between shots of crowded wards and other views of more elves arriving at the hospital. Nick drew a sharp breath but did not interrupt Cyril.

"DJ's tests are inconclusive, but he has been able to get a first look at the virus."

A fuzzy video feed showed a bunch of small particles moving around a group of significantly larger ones.

"He's working to clear the image up now."

"What is it?" asked Nick.

Cyril paused before answering.

"He says it looks like basic bacteria, but it's not. He really has no idea."

The last screen showed a collection of graphs and charts inching toward a 100% infection rate.

"I'll be right there," said Nick.

"Are you sure? What about this doctor?"

"He's not ready yet and I need to see DJ."

Nick reached down and swiped the elfPad screen. The projected monitors vanished and only Cyril's face remained on the elfPad.

"I'm coming in."

"The portable?" asked Cyril.

Nick looked at his briefcase then smiled.

"No. I think I'll check out the lobby."

Cyril looked confused as Nick clicked off the elfPad.

* * *

Back down in the lobby, Nick checked on the progress of the holiday display. The track had been set up and connected, and the train was on the table but not yet on the track. Things had become a little busier at the desk and only a bellboy remained working on the display. He was pulling model buildings from boxes and adding them haphazardly to the display.

One of the women at the reception desk rang the bell to get the bellboy's attention. When she looked over at the display, Nick gave her a wave. She waved back as the bellboy left the display and headed towards her. The woman then turned back to attend to the guests that she was checking in. Nick looked around and once he was sure that no one was watching, he slipped behind the curtain behind the display area. The woman at the reception desk looked up as a soft glow faded behind the curtain, but Nick was already gone.

CHAPTER 12

Things Are Getting Worse

Nick walked briskly down the corridor of the research labs at the medical center. He turned a corner heading toward the main lab and his eyes widened as he saw elves sitting on chairs and lying on gurneys lining the hallway. Despite his shock, he retained his composure, giving an encouraging and confident smile to each elf that caught his eye as he hurried past them. By the time he arrived at DJ's lab at the other end of the corridor, the rows of patients had thinned out. Nick took a deep breath and opened the door to the lab.

The large and well equipped facility was usually handled by DJ himself and a couple of assistants. Today, a small army of white-coated researchers occupied the space.

"There you are."

DJ was standing in front of a large workstation with a scanning electron microscope.

Nick made his way over to DJ.

"Are those all patients in the hallway?" he asked, dreading the answer.

"Yes," replied DJ grimly. "The hospital's full. We're putting patients in here and in a couple of nearby gyms as well."

"What have you found out?"

"It's difficult to explain," said DJ. "Let me show you."

The monitor showed a much clearer picture of the same thing Nick had seen from the hotel room. Large particles were surrounded by a considerable number of much smaller particles.

"What am I looking at?" asked Nick.

DJ shook his head.

"I'm really not sure. The larger cells look just like a common bacteria but somehow have become oversized. The smaller ones we can't identify."

"Oversized?"

"It's like they're swollen, but that's impossible."

Nick watched the screen for a moment. "So, what's the plan?"

DJ's earpiece flashed with an incoming message.

"Yes?"

His face went pale and he looked at Nick as he spoke to the caller.

"We'll be right there," he said and motioned Nick to the door.

"It's Marco!"

* * *

The monitors at Marco's bedside pulsed and beeped in a weak but reassuring rhythm. A couple of other doctors filed out, leaving Nick and DJ alone with Marco.

"Any idea how long?" Nick asked.

DJ chose his words carefully.

"There's no way to know how long a coma will last," he replied before adding gently. "Or how it will end."

Nick nodded.

"He's strong, young,"said DJ.

"Maybe it's that dust," Nick said to himself.

"What?"

"The dust. Remember he fell in the dust at Doc Stevens' layout. It must have something to do with it."

"That's really unlikely."

"I don't know."

Nick was starting to look determined again. He pulled out his phone, selected a number and put his finger to his lips to tell DJ to keep quiet.

"Doctor Stevens," said Nick in a cheery voice. "It looks like I'll be able to make it back tomorrow after all. Yes, the same time would be perfect. "Thanks, I'm looking forward to it."

"I hope this guy is as good as you think he is," said DJ, as Nick ended the call.

"I hope so too," Nick replied. "He might be our only hope."

CHAPTER 13

Cover For Me

"Hi, Dad."

"Hi Vicki," said Doc "Umm, what are you up to this afternoon?"

"Well, I've been alternating between staring at the blank screen on my laptop and poking through notes I'd scribbled down earlier."

"What?" said Doc, not understanding.

"I'm trying to write," she confessed. "You're interrupting my creative process."

"Oh, okay. So you have some time then?"

He wanted that particular process nipped in the bud.

"Dad!"

"Look, Vicki, I need your help. I'm tied up at the lab here for a bit and I need you to cover for me."

"What are you talking about?"

"That Nick fellow called and he's coming back at four. I want you to continue that tour we started yesterday."

"Ah, I told you, I'm trying to write."

Doc thought about that for a moment.

"Well, if you're stuck, maybe you need some help? He is a journalist after all."

"Hmm. That's actually a pretty good idea."

'And I'm sure Jeanette will love it too," Doc added.

"She's out with Helga. They're giving me space to write."

"Okay," said Doc, becoming worried. "Well, are you good to meet with him alone then?"

"Of course. They'll be home soon enough. Oh, and Dad?"

"Yes?"

"Where are all the pictures of Mom?"

"What? Where are you?" he asked, although he had a pretty good idea already.

"I'm using your study to try and write. It's a bit weird with all the pictures gone."

He took a deep breath.

"I couldn't work in there. Too many reminders. I had to take them down. Look, he'll be there soon, and we can talk about this later."

"Okay Dad," said Vicki, sounding disappointed.

"I'll be there as soon as I can."

Doc sighed as he hung up. He'd hoped to get out of the tour entirely but didn't want to leave Vicki alone with someone he didn't really know.

* * *

Nick prided himself on punctuality, and once again managed to arrive precisely at four o'clock.

"Welcome back," said Vicki, as she greeted him at the door. "Come on in."

"Thanks. I'm sorry to do this on such short notice, but I really appreciate you taking the time."

He looked around for the others. As they headed down to the layout Vicki explained. "My Dad has been a bit delayed so I'll have to be your guide again."

Nick smiled.

"So it will be just like yesterday!"

"Except for no trains running today," she said, smiling back at him.

"That'll be fine," said Nick, examining the layout. "I think we left off just below the snowline?"

"That's right."

They moved over to that area and Vicki began the tour in her best narrator voice.

"It's late fall here in the mountains and at these elevations, snow has really started to accumulate. Fortunately, last year, a railcar service was added to take skiers from the main line directly to the base of the ski hill. Unfortunately, it has really been snowing hard up on the hill and the line's been partially blocked by a small avalanche."

She pointed to the scene where a rotary snowplow was grinding through snow piled higher than it's roof.

"It doesn't seem to be bothering the skiers that much," Nick pointed out.

"Well, once they're up here and there's no way out, there's not much they can do about it. The ski lift keeps running and it seems that the ski hill and the resort's patio bar are both in full swing."

Nick shook his head in amazement at the model's detail.

There were pitchers of beer and mugs laid out on the patio. Skiers zipped down the hills and the working ski lift kept hauling them back up the hill for one more run.

He looked at Vicki.

"It's magical!"

"You sound like Jeanette."

"You don't believe in magic?" Nick asked.

"Oh, I don't know," replied Vicki, avoiding the question by moving to the end of the layout. "Then there is... Christmas Town."

Nick waited as she gathered her thoughts.

"This was the first part of the layout that Dad built and it's still my favorite."

They stood in silence and admired the scene together. Tucked in the lee of the mountains, the model town balanced the architecture of many cultures with the charm and wonder of the holiday season. Decorations adorned every house, every building, and even the train station, from which horse-drawn sleigh rides ferried passengers to the town square for the holiday celebrations. The center square was definitely the focus for most of the model townsfolk, featuring a giant Christmas tree and a miniature riding train that circled around it. Everything, everywhere was Christmas. Nick chuckled when the tiny scale train automatically started up and took a load of happy merrymakers for a trip around the tree.

"It's incredible. He's really captured the Christmas spirit!"

"Yes," Vicki agreed, sadly. "I just wish he still felt the same way."

"What happened?" asked Nick.

"My mom was fine, then one day she had a massive brain aneurysm and passed away."

"I'm so sorry."

"It was sudden, unexpected. Not something we could have ever known about. But he blames himself for not seeing it somehow. He's poured himself into his work ever since. He hasn't touched the trains, not until we got here this week." Tears began welling in Vicki's eyes.

"It's been so hard on Jeanette. She knows, but she doesn't really understand the change in him."

"Hmmm," Nick said, thoughtfully. "He hasn't touched his trains until now?"

"Yes," Vicki sniffed, as she got herself under control.

"Well then, that's really very good news."

"What? What do you mean?"

"Well," said Nick, gesturing at the train layout. "I presume you've tried to get him going on this before?"

"Sure, lots of times."

"Well, this time you succeeded. The message got through. That's a sign that he's willing to heal."

And not a moment too soon, Nick thought to himself.

Vicki thought for a moment. Nick saw realization dawn as tears welled in her eyes again. He smiled supportively as she again tried to regain her composure.

"I'm not sure why I'm telling you this. I'm sorry."

"Don't be, Vicki. Sometimes you need to share, and," he said with a wink, "I've been told that I'm a good listener."

"Well, thanks for putting up with me."

She laughed.

"Can I show you something?" she said.

"Of course."

"Over here."

She took him around and showed him a scene just behind Christmas Town where the train track passed by a frozen pond. A lone figure skater was spinning in the center of the pond, while a young man sat watching wistfully from a park bench.

"This is the very first part of the layout that Dad built."

"Is that your mother?" Nick asked.

"Yes," replied Vicki, smiling. "This shows when they first met on the skating pond in the park. Dad said that a steam train had just passed by and had shrouded the rink in steam. He says she just appeared out of the cloud, like magic, spinning in the middle of the pond."

Vicki's eyes misted over and she blinked a few times. She shuffled her feet and Nick grabbed her elbow, steadying her so she wouldn't fall.

"Careful!" he said. "Well. It seems as if you do believe in magic after all."

He supported Vicki while her eyes cleared and she took in their new surroundings. The plastic lady on the pond was now spinning just beside them - exactly the same size that they were! Startled, she looked past Nick and saw Christmas Town looming behind them. It too, was now full size. Vicki gasped as she realized that it hadn't grown. They had shrunk down and were now very small and standing on the layout itself!

CHAPTER 14

A Tiny Tour

"Careful!" Nick chuckled, as he steadied her again. "Take a moment."

"How?" was all Vicki could muster.

Nick smiled warmly.

"Well, as it turns out, if you believe in both the magic of trains and in the magic of Christmas, certain other types of magic also become quite possible."

"And you know this how?" Vicki asked.

Then realization dawned.

"Wait. Nick? As in..."

"Just Nick," he said with another smile. "But now that we're here, why don't we go sit down somewhere and have a chat."

"A chat?"

He looked her straight in the eye.

"I'm not here by chance Vicki. I need your help. Well, actually I need your Dad's help, but I need your help to get him to help. I hope that makes sense? Let's go and sit down."

They walked in silence into Christmas Town. Nick had a pretty good idea how overwhelmed she must be feeling.

"When you're down here, things may seem a little weird."

"You can say that again," said Vicki, as she examined her surroundings.

"What I mean is that what will seem stranger than being small is the sound of being small, or rather, the lack of sound."

They reached the square now and Vicki looked at the plastic people who were gathered round, singing silently. A dog barked, silently. The silence. That was the silence Nick was talking about. Then they were both startled as a loud electric motor shattered the quiet. The model train whirred into life and hauled its cargo of plastic people around the tree in the model town's square once more.

"Okay, that was a bit scary," said Vicki.

Nick just smiled and guided her along.

"Let's try the coffee shop," he suggested.

"If only they had real coffee," Vicki said, as they entered the shop.

"Well, at least they have seats," said Nick.

They slid awkwardly into the plastic chairs on either side of an empty model table. Vicki looked around nervously, still trying to take it all in.

"Here," said Nick, as he offered her a cup of steaming hot cocoa.

"How did you...? Where?"

"Like this."

Nick had his tablet out and was already in the process of extracting a second cup of cocoa for himself. The image on the screen wobbled slightly as the very real cup was extracted from the very flat surface.

"Okay, now that's magic," said Vicki.

"Actually it's not," said Nick.

"But it's an iPad!"

"No," said Nick, correcting her. "It's an elfPad!"

"elfPad?" Vicki parroted.

"Yes," Nick said, matter-of-factly. "Try the cocoa."

"As in elf?" Vicki asked.

"Yes of course. They're the only ones who could pull off this kind of technology."

Vicki looked at him and sipped her cocoa. Her eyes widened as she felt the cocoa energizing her from the inside.

"Wow. What is that?"

Nick smiled.

"Another elf invention. It'll clear your head, give you energy and help you relax, all at once."

Vicki looked anxious.

"Don't worry, it's all natural and not addictive."

Vicki tentatively took another sip then closed her eyes for a moment. When she opened them, she smiled at Nick and got straight to the point.

"So then. Why am I here, with you, sitting on my Dad's train layout?"

"Well, Vicki, we have a big problem. The elves are coming down with something that we can't identify. It's spreading very quickly and we need your Dad's help to try and stop it."

"Okay. Why don't you just ask him?"

"Well, it's a bit tricky. You see, you were able to shrink down because you believe in trains and in Christmas. Since I'm here and somewhat well-practiced, I can help focus what happens with the magic so that we end up where we're supposed to be and be the right size."

"I see," although her tone suggested that she really didn't.
Nick tried to explain things a little better.

"The process only works if you know what you want or
need from the magic. It takes some practice, but it can be taught.
Unfortunately in the case of your dad, right now he doesn't
believe in either Christmas or his trains, so there's no way we
could get him to this size."

"Okay then, why do you need him to be this size?"
Vicki asked.

"Oh, sorry I forgot. Well, right now, you're the size of
an average elf."

"That's crazy!"

Nick shrugged.

"Yet here we are."

Vicki looked intently at their surroundings again. Nick
was glad the cocoa was keeping her level headed.

"Okay, I can accept that. What do you want me to do?"

"You can't just tell him. He simply wouldn't believe
you. He has to come to it on his own."

"This is why you're posing as a reporter, asking about
his trains?"

"That's it exactly. And he's starting to believe again. We
just have to keep things going in that direction."

Vicki shook her head.

"You might get him going on trains, but believing in
Christmas could take a lot longer."

They heard the distinctive sound of the front door of the
house opening upstairs.

Vicki jumped up in panic.

"What do we do?"

Nick reached for her hand.

"Just think about the ice rink, the steam enveloping

your mom and dad, close your eyes and think about a happy Christmas with Jeanette."

And they were standing beside the layout again. Vicki pinched herself to make sure.

"You don't feel anything," Nick told her. "It just happens."

The door at the top of the train room opened.

"Vicki?" Doc called, as he headed down the stairs toward them.

"If I can get him to go with me," Nick whispered. "I may have a way to help him believe, but I'll need your help to convince him."

"Go where?"

"Up North," Nick added quietly under his breath, as Doc cleared the last step.

65

Doc Christmas and The Magic of Trains

CHAPTER 15

The Tour Continues

"How's the tour going?" Doc asked.

"Quite well," replied Nick. "We've been over the major layout features and had a really close look at some of the details."

Vicki had been nodding in agreement but shot Nick an alarmed look when he said that.

"So are we all done then?" said Doc.

"I don't think so," Vicki replied.

"True. Not quite," added Nick. "I'd like to take some pictures and then ask you a few questions. You know, all about the 'man behind the model', that kind of stuff."

Doc sighed and was then embarrassed about being so transparent.

"That would be fine," he said, feigning enthusiasm.

Doc suggested some locations and Nick got out his tablet and took some pictures. He also got a few of Doc and

Vicki with the layout then they all sat down on the workbench stools to do the interview.

"I'll be recording your answers and writing my article later on," said Nick, "but we don't release the audio, so you can say whatever you want. Let's start with the makeup of your layout. Some people model their railroad around a single theme, but you've done things differently. Why?"

Doc thought for a moment.

"This layout was built for me and my family," he said while gesturing at the drawing on the wall, the layout, and Vicki in a wide sweep of his hand. "It wouldn't do that, if it represented only a single region, season, or a specific time period. In fact, it does not even represent a single country. So while it's very possible to view a steam train chugging through the dusty Old West, it is equally possible that a high-speed bullet train may zip by as well."

"I think that's great," said Nick.

"You do?" Doc asked, surprised.

"Sure. You built this for your family and you made it, well, perfect for them!"

Doc was impressed.

"I thought you might be more of a purist."

"Well actually I'm a reporter, but I also happen to be a big fan of trains and I've seen a lot of model trains. There are some great and historically accurate layouts that are wonderful in their own right. From what I've seen so far, you've created a blend of vignettes of moments from different eras and places that blend together in an impressive combination."

Doc was speechless. He'd never really heard it put like that before.

"Thanks."

"Hellooo!"

Their interview was interrupted as Jeanette came rushing

down the stairs, Helga following closely behind.

"Jeanette! Slow down," said Vicki.

"Sorry, Mom. Did I miss the rest of the tour?"

"The tour is over," said Doc, hopefully.

"Almost," Nick corrected him. "I just have a couple more questions."

He turned to Helga.

"I'm Nick."

He offered her a handshake.

"Helga."

"Sorry. Nick, this is Helga," said Doc."She helps me around the house and is helping while Jeanette and Vicki are here as well."

"We went to the museum to see a steam train," said Jeanette, still in awe.

"That sounds nice," Nick said.

"I got to sit in the engine!" Jeanette exclaimed proudly.

"Very nice," said Vicki.

"Helga knows the engineer!" Jeanette whispered to her mom.

Nick looked at Helga quizzically.

"She means Mr. Lundel," Helga explained. "He's the curator of the Museum of Railroad History."

"Okay, you two. Dad and Nick need to finish their interview."

Vicki looked at Jeanette.

"Off you go!"

"Snack Time," said Helga.

Vicki mouthed a silent thank you to Helga, who gave a nod goodbye to them as she wrangled Jeanette upstairs for a snack.

* * *

"How did you get started with trains?" Nick asked.

"I got my first train set when I was a boy," Doc replied. "My dad spent hours helping me learning everything from carpentry for bench work to figuring out how electricity worked so that we could wire it up. Whenever we had to build something from scratch, he helped me learn how to approach the challenge. We'd break it down so it could be dealt with in steps, then we'd learn the steps and pull it all together."

"That's quite a tribute to your dad."

'I guess so," said Doc, then told a white lie. "I built the Christmas section first as a tribute to my Dad. He really loved Christmas."

"Like you used to, Dad."

Doc smiled, sadly.

"Sure. Like I used to."

Doc's head was down, so he couldn't help but notice when Nick's tablet buzzed and showed a picture that had just been texted to him. Doc knew a scanning electron image of bacteria when he saw it. But why would Nick have that?

"What's that?" he asked.

"That is a picture of the problem in my home town."

"What's going on here?" asked Doc, confused. "Who are you?"

"I'm a reporter with *The Northern Times*," Nick replied, then glanced at Vicki. "There's also a problem of some serious proportions underway in my home town."

"He's telling the truth, Dad," said Vicki. "He needs your help."

"And how would you know?" Doc asked.

"He showed me earlier," replied Vicki. "We were trying to figure out how to ask for your help."

"Well, there are channels for this. The CDC, FEMA. There are protocols."

Doc didn't understand why Nick was coming to him.

"Well..." Nick began, then Vicki interrupted him.

"Dad," she said, softly. "He really needs *your* help, not some massive bureaucracy."

Doc shook his head. She knew just how much he hated the red tape and all those well-meaning idiots getting in the way.

"Fine! Let me see that." He held out his hand for the tablet. Nick brought up the picture and handed it to him. Doc studied it for a minute.

"These are bacteria, but I haven't seen this one before. And what are these. It doesn't make sense."

He pointed to the smaller particles in the picture.

"That's exactly what our head researcher said as well," said Nick. "I have video of this and can get you symptom and patient data as well."

"You have video? Of this?"

"Er, yes," said Nick, hesitantly. "Well, I can get it."

"That technology doesn't exist," Doc pointed out. "Unless you're splicing together scans, which is dropping data."

"As far as I know it's a live video feed. It's experimental."

Doc looked at the image, then at Vicki. She gave him an encouraging nod. Perhaps this could get him away from more disruption at home?

"Okay, can you bring your data to my lab?"

"Yes, of course," said Nick, thankfully glancing at Vicki as he added, "I'll need to swing past my hotel first."

"I'll take you," she said.

Doc still thought there was something weird going on, but quickly dismissed it.

"I'll meet you at the lab then. Vicki knows the way."

71

CHAPTER 16

Let's Have a Look

"Grandpa, I like Nick," said Jeanette, as they arrived at Doc's lab.

"He seems nice."

Doc conducted a visual inspection of the office at his lab, double checking that there was nothing dangerous in there at the moment.

"Jeanette, you mustn't touch anything. Your mother would be very upset."

She didn't reply. She was looking behind him.

"Hi, Mom" she said.

Doc turned around. Vicki did not look happy and Nick remained silent.

"Hi Honey. I need to have a word with your Grandpa."

"Don't be mad at him Mom. I made him bring me."

Vicki smiled at her and pulled Doc aside.

"You brought her to the lab?"

"It's completely clear, Vicki. It's safe. I wouldn't have brought her otherwise."

Vicki still looked angry.

"Well, Helga was going out. What was I supposed to do?" Doc protested.

Nick loudly clunked his briefcase down on an empty table and walked over to them.

"I downloaded the video for you," he explained.

Vicki shook her head at Doc once more then gave in. "Fine."

She moved to where she could keep a close eye on Jeanette.

* * *

Nick played the video for Doc. It showed the particles moving around. The bigger ones, the bacteria, seemed passive and the smaller ones were definitely more mobile.

"Hmm, can we put this on a bigger monitor?" Doc asked.

Nick grabbed a cable out of his bag and plugged it into the tablet. He reached behind Doc's computer and clipped his cable onto the monitor cable.

They played the video a couple more times, until Doc noticed something.

"Stop! Go back a bit."

Nick backed the video slightly.

"There!" said Doc. "Do you see it?"

"Er, no."

"Look here," Doc pointed at the screen. "I don't know what those smaller particles are, but this one... Can you run the video slowly?"

Nick nodded.

"This one bumps into and penetrates the cell wall," Doc said excitedly.

"That's bad or good?" asked Nick.

"Well, it's bad, but also good because it's a clue."

Nick just looked puzzled.

"Look, if your people have this technology and haven't figured it out, this might be the clue they need to find it."

"Okay, then that is good," said Nick

"What symptoms are the patients showing?"

"You would need to talk to our head man, but dizziness, disorientation, and at least one has slipped into a coma." Nick's sadness showed in his eyes.

"You need to let them know right away," said Doc.

"They were talking about the bacteria swelling up," Nick added.

"Did they split?"

"I don't think so."

Vicki and Jeanette had been watching silently, listening to the conversation grow more and more technical.

"Dad can you help them?" Vicki finally joined in.

Doc thought about it for a minute. He wasn't sure if he was trying to get out of the family visit or not anymore, but he was pretty sure he could help Nick.

"I think so. Yes, probably. It would be good to see things in person though."

Vicki gave Nick that same odd glance again. Doc wondered what was going on?

"Then you should go," said Vicki.

"It would be wonderful if you could come," Nick added. "Our medical staff would be honored."

"But my family is visiting," said Doc, looking at Jeanette.

"Grandpa," said Jeanette, "if you can help some people, you have to, right?"

"Right, Jeanette. Right."

He started gathering a few things together then stopped and addressed Vicki.

"You sure it's okay if I leave you here for a bit?"

"You go right ahead, Dad. We'll be here."

"Okay. Thanks."

He gave her a smile, a real one, right from the heart. He hadn't done that in a while. It felt good.

"We'll need to get plane tickets," he said to Nick.

"They aren't allowing planes in right now, as a precaution. But the train's still running. It gets there faster than the plane most times anyway. We can catch it at the main station. I think we passed it on the way here?"

"That's right," said Vicki. "It's about halfway home. We can drop you on the way."

As Doc packed up what he needed, he noticed that Nick took the opportunity to whisper something to Vicki.

CHAPTER 17

Northbound Train

The whispering between Nick and Vicki bothered Doc all the way the to the station. His curiosity was about to get the better of him when Nick broke the silence in the car.

"How long until we get there?" he asked.

"Just a few minutes," replied Vicki.

"Why?" Doc asked.

"There's a train leaving in 15 minutes. We'll have to get tickets and board right away as soon as we get there."

Doc did a quick mental check of the gear he'd brought. It should be enough.

Nick wanted to get organized.

"When we get there I can dash in and get the tickets if you're okay with the equipment?"

"No problem," said Doc. "But if you could grab one of the two big cases, that would make it easier."

"Can do," said Nick, as Vicki pulled into the loading zone at the train station.

Nick got out of the car. He looked at Vicki and Jeanette and winked.

"See you soon, ladies. Doc, I'll meet you in the foyer."

"Bye!" Vicki and Jeanette said, in unison.

They quickly helped Doc unload his gear and made sure that he was ready.

"Sorry about running out on you."

"Don't worry, Dad. It's for all the right reasons."

Vicki hugged him then and Jeanette joined in, to make it a family hug.

"Come back soon, Grandpa." Jeanette said.

"I will."

He turned and hurried into the station. The last thing he heard was Jeanette shouting after him.

"I'll look after the trains for you."

* * *

Nick was waiting in the foyer by the time Doc arrived. He held up two tickets in his hand.

"Platform 4. Departs in 6 minutes."

"Guess we'd better hurry then," said Doc.

"Here let me take another," Nick said, reaching for one of the bags.

Together they carried and wheeled Doc's gear through the access tunnel then up to platform 4, right beside the waiting train.

A conductor named Terry, according to his name tag, was waiting there for them.

"Mr. Field?"

"Yes."

"I understand that you need a hand with some special equipment?" the Conductor asked.

"Yes, please. We need to keep it with us, so it can't go in the baggage car. Right, Doc?"

"Right. That would be best."

Terry sighed.

"Okay gentlemen. We're supposed to wait for the porter, but I'd like to get the Northern Explorer out of here on time, so I'll help you load it myself."

"We can do it ourselves," Nick said, as he hopped up with the two bags he was carrying.

Terry grabbed a couple of cases that Doc handed him and headed up after Nick.

"But we do appreciate the help," Nick added.

"I'll show you where to stash them," said the conductor, as he pushed past Nick.

Doc smiled and shook his head as he hoisted up another of the larger cases.

A few minutes later they were all packed on the train and standing outside.

"Thanks for your help, Terry," said Nick.

"No problem. I just like to stay on time."

Terry looked at his watch.

"You best get aboard. I'll be by for your tickets in a bit." He then headed toward the end of the train.

"Nice fellow," Doc remarked.

"Sure is," agreed Nick. "We'd best get aboard."

Doc climbed up first, leaving Nick standing alone at the side of the train. There was nobody else around. Nick reached up and grabbed the stanchion to pull himself onto the train. He put his foot up to the first step, and looked along the outside of the train.

As his foot connected with the car, way up at the front of the train, glowing points of Christmas lights seemed to sprout from the engine, whirled in a curious pattern, then zipped down the length of the entire train, leaving the edges and roofs of all the cars outlined by festive holiday lights.

"Now, that's a Christmas Train," Nick said, smiling to himself.

He had one last look out the door as the whistle blew and the train lurched into motion.

* * *

"Thanks, Terry." Nick said to the conductor as he checked their tickets.

The train rocked gently while the wheels clicked and clacked along.

"You're welcome," Terry replied. "Looks like you have this whole car to yourself tonight."

Doc yawned and Terry winked at him.

"Maybe you can get some sleep."

Terry smiled before moving along to the next car.

"We've got a few hours," Nick said. "Why don't you grab a nap?"

"I'm not really tired. Besides, we should plan what we're going to do when we get there."

"That's a good idea. I'll be back in a minute."

Nick got up and walked down the car until he was out of sight. Nick ducked down in an empty seat, pulled out his elf-Pad and pulled a cocoa out for himself. He changed some settings on the screen, then pulled a second type of cocoa from the screen. He carefully put away the elfPad, picked up both cups and headed back where Doc was sitting.

"Here you go," he said, offering Doc a cocoa.

"Thanks," replied Doc, sniffing the cocoa. "You know, I haven't had this stuff in years."

"It's my favorite."

They toasted and sipped cocoa quietly for a few minutes.

Nick waited until Doc was sound asleep and gently removed the cocoa cup from his hands. Nick watched him sleeping peacefully and smiled.

CHAPTER 18

Above The Pole

A vicious wind whipped the loose snow into a blinding fog that only occasionally permitted glimpses of the rocky outcrops and piled up ice flows. The wind was worse up on the plain above, but still the rusty shell of a quonset hut peeked out from time to time. Tucked under a huge rock face, it had survived the abandonment of the airbase that was now only a memory, it's runways traced out with pieces of scrap and debris. This unnamed secret base had never been shown on any maps. There were no signs proclaiming it's existence. In fact the only thing resembling a sign was a hand painted arrow on the side of the hut itself, which read 'North Pole - 447 km'.

The proximity to the Pole likely explained why the base had been deserted for more than 60 years. Indeed, there wasn't another habitable structure for hundreds of kilometers. It would be impossible to find this place unless you knew exactly where it was. Consequently, a casual observer would have considered it very odd to see the windows of the hut momentarily glow with a soft yellow light, before fading into blackness again.

* * *

The dark station was oppressively cold as Nick helped a groggy, cocoa-sedated Doc along the platform. It was so cold that he wondered if the clouds formed by their breathing would dissipate or freeze solid in midair. There wasn't another soul in sight, as the two of them moved away from the darkened train car with the small pile of bags and equipment sitting on the platform beside it.

"Come on, Doc. It's freezing. Let's get inside."

Nick had to keep holding Doc up as he helped him to the end of the platform.

"Okay," Doc slurred.

"We'll come back for the bags," said Nick, when they reached the end of the platform.

He helped Doc down the steps and through a door. Another stairway in front of them led downwards, illuminated only by a string of dim incandescent lamps. Doc was becoming a little more alert now.

"More stairs? Where are we?"

"Just a few. Down we go."

The temperature warmed as they descended. After about ten minutes of stairs, the frigid atmosphere had given way to something quite bearable. They finally reached the bottom of the stairway where they were confronted by a formidable steel door that looked like it belonged to an old submarine. The red light gleaming over a keypad and retinal scanner beside the door indicated a slightly more recent vintage.

"What's this?" Doc asked, suspiciously.

"Our destination," Nick replied smiling.

He leaned into the scanner. It beeped, then flashed green and the door released with the whoosh of a seal being broken.

A bright light momentarily blinded them as they stepped through the door onto a steel platform.

"Welcome!" said Nick, and he stepped aside.

* * *

They entered an immense, brightly lit cavern. Doc looked up, but the light source was hard to locate as white fluffy clouds obscured it. A flock of birds circled far above and as he watched, a group of them broke formation, dove downwards, then leveled off to soar over the lands below. Doc tried to take it all in, but the height they were viewing from caused him a sudden wave of vertigo. He closed his eyes tightly until it passed.

Doc took a deep breath and opened his eyes, cautiously evaluating their surroundings. He and Nick were on a small steel platform bolted insanely high up on the wall of the huge cavern. A railing that ran around the edge had a viewing telescope on it, similar to the ones found on the roofs of famous skyscrapers. From where they were standing Doc could see towns and villages laid out like patchwork below them. It seemed as if they must be a mile or more up in the sky!

Far off in the distance, a city's towers spiked the skyline. Not too far from the city loomed a massive domed structure. Silvery train tracks connected the towns and villages to the city just like... He squinted and studied the land below more closely. Even though everything seemed far away, Doc felt as if his depth perception must be playing tricks on him. Rather than the cavern being so big and the city and fields so far away, everything actually seemed much smaller and somehow closer?

His vertigo had disappeared. These weren't real towns. Or were they? The perspective was off. It didn't seem high, yet they were so far above the ground, or were they? Doc turned to Nick, who had been patiently waiting.

"What is this?" Doc asked. "Where are we?"

"Welcome," Nick said. "To the North Pole."

CHAPTER 19

Lookout Below

"The North Pole?" Doc said, incredulously.

"Yes," replied Nick. "Sorry to spring this on you."

Doc looked around again.

"The North Pole?"

"Well, technically it's about 400 kilometers, that way," said Nick, pointing to his right. "But, yes, this is the North Pole that you probably think it is."

Doc looked straight down and immediately experienced vertigo again. He looked at Nick.

"We're not a mile high, are we?"

Nick laughed.

"No, we're not."

"So everything down there is small? A model?"

"Small yes, a model, no," Nick replied, pointed to just behind Doc. "Look here."

With the grand scale of the world below him, Doc had completely failed to notice that the platform they were on also held a tiny structure. It looked similar to the upper level of the chair lift model on his layout, but this one was built to handle a gondola. In fact, there was one in the station waiting to begin its descent. Doc got down on his hands and knees. There was a coffee shop and a small viewing area. It didn't look like a model at all. It looked so real. He even heard a small sound as the tiny cappuccino machine emitted a puff of steam.

Doc got to his feet and steadied himself against the railing. "Okay, so... not a model."

"Elves are very small," Nick said, matter-of-factly. "This is their world. They look like us, they live like us, they're just... a whole lot smaller than we are."

"So the city?" Doc asked.

Nick looked Doc up and down.

"Is probably just a bit taller than you, some of the buildings anyway."

"What's it called?" Doc asked.

"Just the City," Nick replied as he turned and pointed out some areas below. "Behind it is the Workshops area and that big building with the dome is the Hub. The Hospital's in that area as well."

"The Hospital?"

"The elves are sick," said Nick, his tone becoming more serious now. "There really is an epidemic. That's why I brought you here."

Doc looked at the gondola station, then at his hands, and then at Nick. "But what can I do? I can't work on something or someone that small!"

"That's why we're up here on the platform for now. You can't go crashing around down there. The way North Pole magic works is tricky. I can use my magic to help get you here, but to get you down there, to get you to 'fit' in, well, you'll have to do that part yourself."

"I highly doubt that will happen," Doc said, skeptically.

"I don't know, Doc. There was a time when you could have easily done it. You see it's all about the magic of Christmas and the magic of trains. Something happens when you believe in both. You're able to become the size of an elf and vice versa."

"Okay," said Doc, although he had no idea where all this was going.

"Well, your love of trains is coming back, thanks in part to your family's visit. But the love of Christmas, enough to get you down there, is going to be difficult. You see, Christmas means many things to many people, but there's one thing at its core, wherever you find it."

Nick walked across to the viewing telescope and looked through it, searching for something.

"Do you know what that is?"

"I don't... No, I don't know," Doc replied hesitantly.

Nick found what he was looking for. He beckoned Doc over to the viewfinder.

"Have a look."

Doc looked through the eyepiece as Nick said softly in his ear.

"Your daughter knows," he said. "And Jeanette too."

Doc saw a frozen pond through the scope. A young woman pirouetted in the middle of the ice as a young girl skated around her. Nick waved from the platform beside Doc. Both the skaters looked up and waved back. There was no mistaking Vicki and Jeanette,

Doc's eyes misted over. He looked at Nick.

"They're here? But how?"

"The common thing is love."

Doc closed his eyes holding back the tears.

"But I've been pushing them away..."

"I know," said Nick. "They feel your pain. They lost Marilee too. But they're your family and they love you. They couldn't have made it here if they didn't believe."

Doc looked at Nick and smiled. He blinked away a couple of tears, clearing his eyes. Nick was pointing up. High above them the viewscope still pointed towards the skating pond, but there was no way they could reach it now. At the size they had just shrunk to, they were simply too small.

CHAPTER 20

Down To Business

Doc and Nick made their way across the steel decking to the gondola. What had been a few feet only moments ago was now the equivalent of several hundred yards. The embossed fishplate patterns, as Doc found out the hard way, were now curb height and could easily be tripped over.

"This is very strange," he said, picking himself up.

"The first time is the best!" agreed Nick.

"I'm not sure that's what I meant," Doc said, before grinning at Nick.

"Lets stop at the coffee shop," Nick suggested, gesturing Doc to head inside.

"Pull up a stool, Doc," said Nick, as he sat at the coffee bar. "What would you like?"

"What do you have?" asked Doc, taking his seat.

A tall blond fellow with vaguely Nordic features chose

that moment to pop up from behind the cappuccino machine.

"Have a Cocoa 47," he said quickly.

Doc was so startled that he fell off his stool. Nick smiled and helped him up.

"Doc, this is Fetna. He runs the gondola and takes care of most of our aerial work, here and in the Hub."

"Pleased to meet you, Doc," said Fetna, speaking just a bit faster than Doc thought was normal. "Sorry about surprising you."

Doc then noticed the silvery earpieces that Fetna was wearing.

"You're an elf?" he asked.

"Sure am. Here's your Cocoa 47."

He handed Doc a steaming mug and then steamed a cappuccino for Nick.

"No cocoa Nick?" Doc asked, as he had a sip from his drink.

"I don't need any. But watch out, it's got a kick."

Seconds later, Doc was simultaneously getting relaxed, energized and refreshed with the effects of the Cocoa 47. "What is this?" he asked.

"That, my friend," replied Fetna, "is the good stuff."

"Think of it as an all-natural energy drink with no side effects," Nick added.

"Okay," said Doc "Thanks for the cocoa, Fetna."

"No problem."

"You live up here?" Doc asked.

"It's quiet up here," replied Fetna. "Usually."

"And you're one of the few who aren't afraid of heights," Nick added.

"There's that," said Fetna, nodding.

"Fetna runs the gondola, mans the upper galleries at the Hub, and generally handles anything that requires heights. Most elves are uncomfortable with heights."

"Does the gondola get much traffic?" asked Doc, looking around.

"No," Fetna replied smiling. "Hence the quiet."

"I see," said Doc, before changing the subject. "Nick, what makes this whole shrinking thing work?"

Fetna rolled his eyes while Nick laughed.

"That's a loaded question," said Nick. "The elves have been working on that for many, many years."

"We've been trying to understand it for centuries," Fetna added. "We don't know why the magic works, just how it works!"

"Forgive me Fetna," said Nick. "That's what I meant. They've been trying to figure it out for a very long time, but so far magic is magic, and science is science."

"Okay then. How does it work?" Doc pressed.

"Basically, you need three things to make it work," replied Nick. "If you believe in Christmas in your heart, if you have a need to be smaller...".

"Or larger." Fetna added.

"Or larger," Nick continued, nodding, "and if you believe it can be done, then you can do it."

"And once you've done it a few times..." Fetna added.

He quickly ran out of the coffee shop onto the open steel decking.

"Showoff," Nick called after him.

Fetna was instantly the huge, albeit normal, size that Doc and Nick had been earlier.

"Remember the pond scene on your layout?" Nick asked him. "Vicki told me it was a special Christmas memory for you. You probably spent hours creating it, making it just right, When you do things like that, you're tapping in to your creative side, but also accessing a special kind of magic. When you saw Vicki and Jeanette skating on that pond, you accessed that memory and that magic, so you were able to shrink."

Fetna looked through the viewscope and waved to the girls on the pond. He gave them an A-OK sign with his thumb and forefinger, then moved closer to the coffee shop and shrunk back down again.

"It becomes easier," said Nick. "Like muscle memory almost. With a little practice it's almost automatic.

"Now can we go?" asked Fetna as he ran up to them.

"Go?" asked Doc, still trying to process all the magic information.

"We have an epidemic to cure," Nick reminded him.

"Right," said Doc. "How long does the gondola take?"

"About 20 minutes," Fetna replied with a smile. "I was thinking of something faster."

Nick nodded.

"Right this way!"

Fetna hurried out. Doc and Nick followed him around to the back of the building, where an opening garage door faced toward the edge of the platform, connected by what looked suspiciously like a runway. A sound that resembled muted turbine engines could be heard from inside the garage. Seconds later Fetna floated out of the garage in a sleek vehicle that hovered about a foot off the ground.

As sleek as a Lamborghini, the open-top design revealed a couple of leather covered bench seats and a simple control panel. The way the back of the craft was designed, it looked like it could be opened to hold cargo, or extended forward to enclose and cover the passenger compartment. The cherry red paint job did nothing to diminish the impression that this vehicle was designed to go very, very quickly.

"Hop in!" said Fetna.

"This is a flitter, Doc," said Nick. "Very versatile, but we rarely use them."

"Why?" asked Doc as he settled into the seat.

Fetna looked over his shoulder and grinned at Doc mischievously.

"Buckle up!" warned Nick.

Fetna inched the flitter slowly forward until it was completely clear of the platform.

"They can get a little exuberant with them," said Nick, with a shrug.

Fetna touched the controls and the flitter dropped like a stone. He pulled the drop into an arc that curved them around until they shot straight up towards the clouds. Leveling off, he descended again, this time performing a series of seemingly random turns and maneuvers, all the while gaining more and more speed. Eventually they settled down to a pace that Doc felt could be best described as 'far too fast', zipping across the landscape as they headed for the city.

CHAPTER 21

Elven Hospital

"Hang on! Quick stop!" Fetna advised as they reached the outskirts of the city.

He pointed the flitter's nose straight up and cut power. They shot upwards until their vertical momentum slowly surrendered to gravity. Once they'd stopped rising, Fetna leveled off and the craft went into free fall until he eventually turned the engines back on to slow their descent.

"That's an interesting way of slowing down." Doc said. 'Why am I not, um, terrified?"

"Given the capabilities of a flitter, that's the most time-efficient stop possible," Fetna replied. "Slowing down earlier would take approximately three times as long."

Nick was texting someone at the hospital and didn't even look up, but he answered the rest of Doc's question. "Cocoa 47."

"That is some interesting cocoa!" said Doc, shaking his head.

Doc had no idea how he had done it, but Fetna had timed their rate of descent and trajectory perfectly. They'd slowed gradually from a free fall until, as their vertical velocity approached zero, Fetna had settled the Flitter precisely into one of the VIP parking spots at the hospital.

"Let's go," said Nick, as he helped Doc down from the flitter. "Fetna, can you collect the Doc's gear from the train platform?"

"Sure can."

He fired up the engines and when Nick and Doc were clear the flitter lifted straight up. Fetna then sped away, but instead of going towards the platform, he headed further away from the direction they had come from.

"Isn't he going the wrong way?" Doc asked.

Nick simply shrugged and turned toward the hospital entrance. A small group of people in white coats stood there waiting for them.

As Nick and Doc walked over to the entrance, Doc glanced back over his shoulder. He thought he saw the flitter descending close to the large domed structure. When they arrived at the door they were surrounded by white coated, sparkly-eared elves.

"Doctor Stevens," said Nick. "This is Doctor Jay, our head physician."

"I usually go by DJ," Doctor Jay said, as he and Doc shook hands.

Doc noticed that DJ spoke quite quickly as well. He wondered if it was an elf trait?

"Nice to meet you, Doctor, I mean DJ. Most people just call me Doc."

"A pleasure to meet you Doc," replied DJ, waving at

the half dozen other elves around him. "These are a few other people that you will need to meet later. Can we get started?"

"Sure. I..." Doc began, before DJ quickly continued.

"First, let me assure you that we take every precaution to prevent transmission. Nothing is really necessary for you however because the virus doesn't affect humans and all the elves are affected already."

"What? You all have it?" Doc asked, flabbergasted.

"That appears to be the case," replied DJ. "Right this way."

"When did this all start?" Doc asked as they moved into the hospital lobby.

Before DJ could answer him, Doc stopped in his tracks. The lobby resembled the lobby of a large corporation or fancy municipal building. Wide sweeping staircases and ramps led up to big airy corridors and huge interior green spaces. However, every inch of the building was packed with gurneys, wheeled hospital beds, even rows of chairs, all with sick elves on them. It was a triage nightmare come to life.

"You're all sick?" Doc asked again.

'To be honest, sickness isn't something that happens that often here," DJ explained. "The hospital is simply not designed for this many patients. There are elves here, in the labs, and in gyms nearby."

"We'd better go to the lab then. You said there are patients there as well?"

"Yes," DJ replied.

Nick was on his phone.

"Okay, perfect. Thanks," Nick said, before hanging up.

"Doc, your gear is at DJ's lab."

"That was fast," Doc remarked.

"Excellent, lets go!" said DJ.

One of the other doctors handed Doc an elfPad, and

began showing him how to use it. DJ said goodbye to Nick, then the whole group turned and started off down the hallway, talking as they headed to the lab.

Recognizing that he really wouldn't be of any use at the lab, Nick remained in the lobby.

"I'll go and show the girls around," he called after Doc.

After a few encouraging words here and there amongst the sick elves that caught his eye, Nick walked out of the hospital. The flitter was right where Fetna had parked when they'd first arrived. Nick hopped aboard, fired up the engine and headed for the skating rink.

CHAPTER 22

Touring The Pole

Vicki and Jeanette were sitting on the bench changing out of their ice skates when Nick walked over from where he'd parked the flitter.

"Hello!" he called out as he approached, not wanting to startle them.

"Hi," replied Vicki. "Well, that seemed to work."

"It worked perfectly!" said Nick.

"Grandpa's going to help you now?" Jeanette asked.

Nick smiled at her. "He already is Jeanette. Thank you so much for helping."

"What did I do?"

"You came here, honey," said Vicki. "And we helped Grandpa remember."

"Remember what?" Jeanette asked.

"Remember who he is," replied Vicki.

Jeanette thought for a moment.

"Does that mean we'll get a Christmas tree now? Like Grandma Marilee used to do? "

Vicki looked unsure, but Nick winked at her.

"Yes," said Nick." I think it does, Jeanette."

"Yay!"

"It's cause for celebration, for sure," said Nick. "How would you like to go to the candy store?"

"Yes, please!" Jeanette exclaimed.

"Vicki? Cocoa? Cappuccino?" Nick asked.

"Either would be lovely."

"Well then, let's go," said Nick.

"In that?" Jeanette asked, nervously pointing at the flitter.

"What's wrong honey?" said Vicki.

"It goes too fast!" Jeanette replied, looking scared.

"Were you watching when we took your Grandpa to the lab?" Nick asked.

Jeanette nodded.

"I see. We went really fast didn't we?"

She nodded again.

"When Fetna dropped you off here at the pond before, did he go fast?" Nick asked.

Jeanette shook her head.

"Well, we're not in a hurry to get to the candy store are we?"

"No," Jeanette agreed.

"So it will be okay if I don't go fast?"

"Yes. But... Nick?"

"Yes?"

"You don't have to go *too* slow either." Jeanette added.

* * *

Situated in a bedroom community on the outskirts of the elven city, the candy store looked like a supermarket from the outside but it's interior was laid out like a wine store. Candies from all over the world were displayed in sections marked by the name of their country of origin. Jeanette found a few familiar things and Nick suggested some local delights for her to try. They hadn't seen anyone in the entire store, but when they got to the front, a friendly looking lady with silvery ear ornaments greeted them. Her name tag read 'Mary' and she scanned their purchases for them.

"Here you are, Miss," said Mary as she handed Jeanette the bag of candy.

"Thank you," Jeanette replied politely.

"Enjoy your stay!" Mary added, as they left.

Outside the door, Jeanette carefully waited until they were out of earshot.

"Is Mary an elf?" she asked Nick.

"Why yes she is! How did you know."

Jeanette shrugged off the question.

"It was the ear decorations, right?" said Vicki, while glancing at Nick.

"Yes," Jeanette replied. "I tried not to stare. I didn't want to be rude!"

"Oh, I wouldn't worry about that!" said Nick, laughing.

"What do you mean?" Jeanette asked.

"Those are her Eyralin. They have a functional Elf-Tec core but the design is very personal and elves pride themselves on their Eyralin. If you'd mentioned them, it would have been a big compliment. Well, as long as you liked them!"

Nick winked.

"They were beautiful," said Jeanette.

"Well, you'll know for next time," Vicki added. "Nick, I don't mean to be rude, but we didn't pay for the candy and we..."

103

"No, No, don't worry," Nick interrupted her. "We don't use money here."

"But Mary scanned our purchases?" said Vicki.

"That's just inventory control. Elves are pretty sticky about that."

"So how does that work?" Vicki asked.

"Well, it's a closed society. Everything you put in or take out is logged. If you take out too much, you get assigned extra work. It doesn't happen very often."

"What if you put in too much?" Vicki asked.

"That can be more interesting. There's always a bit of a competition to see who has put in the most extra. It's a matter of pride, I think."

"How much work will I have to do for my candy?" Jeanette asked, seriously.

Nick laughed loudly.

"Well, Jeanette since you are all our guests here, you don't have to worry about that. I'm sure you actually do have an account, but the help your Grandpa is providing will far outweigh any amount of candy you could ever eat."

"I don't know about that," said Vicki smiling. "She can eat a lot of candy!"

"Mom!" Jeanette scolded her.

"Okay, enough on that subject," said Nick, laughing. "Cocoa or cappuccino, Vicki?"

"I'm a bit tired," Vicki replied. "So maybe..."

"Cocoa then," said Nick.

"That would be perfect."

They sat down at a picnic table in the center of the small town where the candy store was located. Nick got out his elfPad and poured a cocoa for Vicki and himself while Jeanette happily sampled her candy. The town square looked like it should be a busy place, but there were very few people around.

"Where is everybody?" Vicki asked. "It seems so quiet."

"Most everybody is sick," replied Nick.

"What?"

"That's why we need your Dad's help."

"We should go and help him," said Jeanette.

"That's kind of you, Jeanette, but even I am not needed there right now. We have to let the experts do their jobs."

He changed the subject.

"So, I believe we were going to have a tour?"

"That sounds nice," said Vicki.

* * *

They took off from the road in the flitter and floated above the picturesque community. From the air, it looked like any other town. A river ran through the center of town, a train track running along its bank. Nick showed them schools, shops, and picturesque houses of all styles before they arrived at the city.

Like everything else they'd seen, the city was both old and new, a combination of modern and traditional styles from around the world. Yet every aspect of the eclectic mix was dwarfed by the huge shiny Elf-Tec Tower.

"What is Elf-Tec?" Vicki asked. "You mentioned it before."

"Elf-Tec is just like it sounds. They make the best technical equipment anywhere. Most of the high-tech gadgets you have out in the real world were invented right here, or at least the underlying technologies were."

"Wow!" said Vicki.

Nick swooped the flitter around the Elf-Tec building one more time then showed Vicki and Jeanette a little more of the city. Just beyond the towers were the Workshops, rows of low industrial buildings that fanned out for quite a distance behind the city. The Workshops were flanked by store piles and warehouses full of raw materials. Beyond that, the temperature warmed slightly, and the scenery gave way to rolling hills with orchards, fields, and towns interspersed all the way down to the edge of the underground ocean, that vanished into the distance.

"What's that?" asked Jeanette, pointing at puffs of white smoke coming from a wooded area they hadn't been over yet.

"Let's have a look," Nick replied, as he veered the flitter to investigate.

"Could it be a steam train?" Vicki asked.

"Definitely," said Nick. "It looks like the Lake Train headed back to the city. It's a duplicate of the Carmangie Flyer, which is from your neck of the woods, I think."

The rhythmic chuffing of the steam engine was soothing, even from above.

"I wish Helga could see this," said Jeanette. "She loves steam trains."

"Well, maybe we should go for a ride?" Nick suggested. "What do you think, Vicki?"

"Sure, if we have time."

'We should. I'll flag them down."

* * *

The flitter was the probably the best tour vehicle ever designed. It could hover at any level or dash around as fast as one might wish to travel. Nick dropped down and glided alongside the train, approaching it from behind. As they neared the engine. Nick thought something looked a little unusual. He was about to say something to Vicki, who had a better view from her side of the flitter, when...

"He's unconscious!" Vicki yelled. "The engineer looks like he's unconscious!"

"That's not good!"

Nick maneuvered around to get a better look. The engineer was slumped over at the controls.

"Really not good! Vicki, grab the stick."

"What!"

"Grab the stick," Nick repeated. "I need to get over there. You'll need to fly the flitter."

"But I can't fly anything."

"It's easy," he said, smiling at her confidently. "Just hold it steady. Once I'm over there, I'll give you a thumbs-up and you can punch this button. That puts the flitter into training mode and it will become much easier to fly. In that mode, it'll almost fly itself."

"I don't know."

"I need your help Vicki. Can you help us too, Jeanette?" She nodded.

"Once I'm in," Nick continued, "I'll stop the engine and give you a thumbs-up. You tell your mom and make sure she pushes this control."

He pointed to a button that read 'Land'.

"Okay," said Jeanette, bravely.

"Okay," Vicki added, though she looked far from confident.

Vicki slid over and took the controls. Nick quickly showed her what to do then watched the train closely.

"This will all be done in a minute or two," he said. "But I will need you to get a bit closer to the train."

Vicki slid the craft gingerly over. Nick nodded at them, glowed, and was gone.

"He's in the train!" Jeanette yelled.

Vicki pushed the first button and the flitter went into training mode.

The regular puffing of steam soon changed tempo then steel screeched on steel as Nick applied the brake. The train was definitely slowing now. Vicki was losing her fear of the flitter and was even smiling a bit. Jeanette kept a watchful eye on the train.

"He's waving," she yelled. "Press the other button."

The flitter slowed and the vehicle almost seemed to be checking its surroundings as it prepared for it's descent.

They landed not far from the train. Nick had already extracted the crew and was checking the engineer and conductor while they were lying on the grass. They were both groggy and semi-conscious at best.

"Help me get them into the flitter," said Nick.

He and Vicki loaded the two elves into the flitter and Nick climbed inside to make sure that they were strapped in securely. Nick called the hospital on his elfPad and let them know the injured elves would be arriving soon. He then set the flitter to automatic, and hopped out.

"What are you doing?" asked Vicki.

"Well," Nick replied as he reached in pushed the 'Go' button. "These fellows need attention, but someone also has to shut down the train properly."

They all watched as the flitter gently took off then headed off in the direction of the hospital.

"Steam trains have to be handled carefully and I didn't think you were quite ready to fly them to the hospital," Nick explained with a reassuring smile. "Don't worry. We use automatic all the time. They'll be fine."

He crouched down and looked at Jeanette.

"That was quite an adventure!"

She nodded slowly.

"Do you think you could handle one more adventure today?"

"I think so," said Jeanette.

"Somebody has to take this train home, and it looks like it will have to be us. Do you think we can handle that?"

"It sounds like you think we can," said Vicki.

"Ok" Jeanette added, her eyes wide.

They hopped aboard the train and Nick propped his elf-Pad up in front of him. He linked in with railroad control and reported what had happened. He also asked if a crew could meet them at the hospital station and take over the train. After everything was confirmed, Nick asked dispatch to clear them a route. Once he received the route map on his elfPad, he released the brakes, added water to the boiler, and slowly pulled back the throttle. The train lurched slightly and they began to chug along.

They had been routed through the countryside to avoid any traffic problems with the Workshops and the City. They didn't see any other trains along the way, so they had the most uneventful and relaxing trip possible all the way to the hospital. They got to see much of the landscape that they'd seen from the air but at a much more leisurely pace. Everything was even more breathtaking at close range.

When the train finally arrived at the hospital station, Nick, Vicki and Jeanette hopped out and a train crew took over. They gave a couple of toots of the whistle as the train pulled away. Once it had cleared the station, they found themselves standing at the back of the hospital. When they walked around to the front entrance, Vicki and Jeanette were relieved to see that the flitter was parked there.

CHAPTER 23

About The Hub

Doc was waiting for them with DJ just outside the hospital doors. Doc was quite concerned as he ran over, but his worry lessened when he saw that Vicki and Jeanette were okay, and were even laughing and chatting with Nick about their adventure.

"Vicki!"

"Dad! What..."

Her sentence was cut off as Doc hugged her.

"I heard that there was a problem with the flitter, and something to do with a train?" asked Doc.

"We're fine, Grandpa," Jeanette explained. "Mom flew the Flitter! And Nick was the engineer on the steam train."

"We had a bit of an adventure but we're all fine," added Vicki.

"They did a great job and helped prevent a possible

accident," said Nick. "You should be proud of them."

'I am. You'll have to tell me all about it later," said Doc. "Right now I need to get back to my lab to run some tests."

"Did you find something?" Nick asked.

"Doctor Stevens has a couple of ideas we hadn't thought of," said DJ, as he joined them. "And since he has the equipment to run the tests, it may be quicker for him to run them there."

"DJ said that we can get back much easier than, well, how we got here. Is that right?" Doc asked.

"Much easier!" said Nick, laughing. "Do you have what you need?"

DJ beckoned over one of the other doctors who handed Doc a small case.

"Yes, it's all here."

Doc reached out and shook DJ's hand.

"You do some amazing things here. I'm sure we can beat this thing by working together."

"A pleasure, Doctor, I mean Doc," DJ said, handing him an elfPad. "Take this. You can use it to keep in touch wherever you are."

After everyone said their goodbyes, Nick loaded them all into the flitter and took off again, this time they headed towards the massive domed building. Nick pointed out features to Jeanette as they travelled.

"So how did you two get here?" Doc asked.

Vicki paused for a moment before she answered.

"Because I'd already shrank down during the layout tour, Nick knew..."

"What?" Doc asked.

"Don't interrupt, Dad. Anyway, Nick knew I could do it and also knew Jeanette would have no problem. So he asked me to bring her down to the layout when I got back from the train station."

"Okay," said Doc.

"When we got there, Fetna was waiting for us by your layout. Nick had sent him. He explained we were going on a trip and, well, we just shrank down onto your layout and climbed aboard one of your model trains."

"What?" said Doc, confused. "Then what?"

"Then we got off the train. Here, at the Hub."

Vicki gestured to the large dome that they were about to land beside.

* * *

Nick settled the flitter down on the roof of the main building, right next to the dome. He powered down and everyone hopped out.

"Normally we go through the front door, but this is closer to the control room," he explained. "Vicki and Jeanette, I don't think you had time to see all this before either."

He opened the double doors with a flourish.

"This is the Hub," he said with pride as he ushered them inside.

It seemed very dark inside, but once the doors had closed, they were able to make out details on the holographic globe. It seemed to be divided into time zones and there were points of different colored lights sprinkled all over the globe. As they walked around the central platform and down the stairs, Nick offered an explanation.

"During the Industrial Revolution, the population of the world grew so quickly that our traditional distribution methods weren't keeping up. The elves discovered quite by accident that trains, the very thing that made the Industrial Revolution possible, also had a type of magic to them. Since then, we've been using the magic of trains along with the magic of Christmas to deliver Christmas."

As he led them down the stairs to the main platform, he continued. "The map shows believers and non-believers all over the world. The blue lights are portals."

"Train portals, to be exact," Cyril added, clearing his throat as he turned from his console.

"Cyril is our head elf," Nick said.

"And I'll be the one using those train portals to get you home today," added Cyril as he swiveled back to his monitor. "Briefcase?"

"Briefcase," Nick confirmed.

Cyril flipped through a collection of images that were displayed on his screen until he came to one that looked quite similar to the briefcase that Nick had left in Doc's office. Cyril selected the image and pointed up at a newly blinking blue light on the map.

"There you go," he said, pressing a few more buttons.

Down below, alarm bells rang as the transport car below them began reconfiguring.

"What are you doing?' Jeanette asked.

Cyril spun around and smiled at her.

"I am reconfiguring the inside of that train car down there to match this train right here."

He pointed at the picture of the briefcase on his screen.

"Is that where we're going?" asked Vicki.

"That's where we're going through," said Nick "Don't worry, I'll come along to make sure everything's okay."

They all went down to the track and hopped aboard the train car. It seemed tighter and more cramped than they would have expected for a train car, and it had odd protrusions between the seats and on the walls where there usually wasn't anything. Some seats were filled in completely and the open seats were oddly shaped so that the adults had to squeeze to get into them.

Jeanette laughed, she thought it was funny.

"Why is it so tight in here?" asked Vicki.

"Watch," said Nick, pointing out the window.

They looked out the window, where they could see the train tracks and platforms of the Hub. As they kept watching, the window seemed to glow for a moment and when the glow faded they had a window with a view of Doc's lab office!

The surfaces they were sitting on had changed too. The seats had become lumps of plastic, and the view through the windows was now distorted by the sheer thickness of plastic window panes.

"So we're on another model train?" asked Vicki.

"A T-gauge train," Nick replied. "The briefcase I left in your office holds a T-gauge train set, which we are now on, or rather, in."

"I've never heard of T-gauge," said Doc. "What's that?"

Nick began to ease open the train's door.

"It should stand for tiny," said Nick. "But..."

As soon as he opened the door fully they all glowed and then were standing full size again, just in front of the briefcase.

"...it means 3mm," Nick explained. "That's the distance between the rails."

Nick picked up the train car they had just been in. It was just about the thickness of a pencil.

"We were in there?" said Jeanette, incredulously.

"Sure were," Nick replied.

"Wow," said Jeanette, as she checked out the rest of the tiny layout.

Nick set the train car back on the track.

"I'm going to head back and see what I can do to help out."

"But," Jeanette began looking sad.

"Don't worry, I'll see you all very soon. Thank you for your help. Use the elfPad to reach us!"

He glowed and vanished. A moment later the train car glowed briefly and Doc and the others knew he was gone.

CHAPTER 24

Back at Doc's Lab

After Nick left, Doc opened the blinds on the window behind his desk. Morning sunlight streamed into the lab. Surprised, he checked the clock on his computer.

"9:00 AM. Hmm, right," he said. "I've got to get to work."

"We were up all night?" Vicki asked.

Doc shrugged.

"I feel fine. Must be that cocoa."

"I'm not tired either," said Jeanette, yawning.

Vicki smiled at her.

"Really? Well, maybe we'll go see if we can nap for a bit anyway. Just in case."

"But, Mom."

"Ladies," Doc intervened. "I have a lot of work to do and I'm afraid there isn't much that you can do to help right now. Jeanette, thank you for everything you've done so far, but right now I need you to take your mom home."

He then whispered in Jeanette's ear.

"I think she might need a nap."

"Okay, Grandpa."

"We'll call you later," said Vicki, as she hugged Doc goodbye, adding with her own whisper. "Thank you."

"Make the elves better, 'K?" Jeanette added, as Vicki ushered her out the door.

"I'll do my best," said Doc.

Once they were gone, Doc sat down at his desk for a moment and reflected on everything that had happened in the previous 12 hours. He smiled to himself as a tear rolled down his cheek. He wiped it away, and reached for the elfPad and the sample case. He brought up the picture of the bacteria that DJ had isolated.

"Now, let's see if we can find out what you are."

Walking into the inner lab, Doc started the power up sequence on the electron microscope and began preparing slides for reaction testing. Then he set the centrifuge running to see if he could precipitate those tiny cells that remained unidentified. He unlocked an insulated cabinet and selected a tray full of chemical and antibacterial agents. The centrifuge beeped to indicate that it had stopped so he decided to start with that.

Under the microscope, it appeared that the centrifuge had not worked in isolating the small cells. He set it to run for even longer this time, then started logging entries in his laptop, as well as inputting data into the mainframe attached to the microscope.

He set up the tray of agents, the slides he had set up and the samples from the North Pole, then sat down in front of the microscope. He selected the first agent and made a log entry for it on his laptop and into the mainframe. He loaded a microsyringe with the agent and another with some of the sample. He placed the slide in the microscope, deposited a drop of the sample on the slide and scanned for it. When he had it in focus, Doc added a microdot of the agent and waited for a reaction. After ten minutes of observation nothing had happened. He set the slide to one side, made some notes, and selected the next agent from the tray.

* * *

A couple of hours and dozens of samples later, a door chime alerted Doc that someone was entering his office. He turned and saw through the lab window that Vicki and Jeanette had come in. They were waving a paper bag at him.

"Turns out she wasn't sleepy after all!" said Vicki, over the intercom.

"We brought you breakfast," Jeanette added.

"I'll be out in a couple of minutes," said Doc.

When the current batch finished, Doc made a note of the time, completed his entries and left the lab. Vicki had laid out a spread of breakfast delights.

"How's it going?" she asked.

"Just getting started," Doc replied, as he selected an english muffin. "Thanks for bringing breakfast!"

"Helga said you probably wouldn't eat if someone didn't bring something," said Vicki. "She was going to come herself."

"Helga!" Doc chided himself. "She's coming in this week. I forgot all about her."

"She's okay," Jeanette said between bites. "Mom told her what happened."

"You what?" said Doc, in alarm.

"I told her all about the problem with the steam engine," Vicki explained. "How we all helped out and how it took the whole night to get everything settled."

She smiled mischievously.

"I may have left out who we were with, where we were, and a few other details."

"Mom was sneaky," Jeanette added, with a giggle.

"I'm sure I'll be grilled at length about that at some point," said Doc grinning. "Meanwhile, nice save."

Jeanette had climbed up on a chair and was looking into the lab.

"So what do you have to do, Grandpa?"

"Well, I'm trying to find out two things," Doc began as he came up behind her. "First, what is it that made the elves sick and second, is there anything that makes the sickness sick."

He hoped that would suffice, but he could see Jeanette's wheels turning.

"How?" she asked.

Doc looked at Vicki for help, not really expecting any, but this time, she came to his rescue.

"Honey, Grandpa needs to do the work, rather than tell you about it. You want the elves to get better, right?"

"Of course."

"Then let's give him time do his work and he can tell you about it later, when they're better."

"Okay. Sorry, Grandpa."

"Jeanette. I'll be happy to tell you all about it when there's more time. Once these tests are done, I tell the computer all about it and then it tries to find things that will help me."

Jeanette looked confused.

"You see, while it's thinking about things I can go home and get some sleep. Maybe I'll have some time to tell you then too. Will that be okay?"

"That will be nice Grandpa."

"Okay, lets go, missy," said Vicki. "Bye Dad."

They both gave Doc a quick hug before turning to leave.

"Bye, Grandpa."

"Bye, girls."

* * *

Six hours later, he'd finished testing all the agents and had logged all the results into the mainframe. The centrifuge wasn't yielding any results so he turned it up another notch, setting the timer for four hours this time. He called DJ on the elfPad to exchange updates.

"Hi, Doc," said DJ, his voice sounding weak." How's it going?"

"DJ, you don't sound so good."

"Many are worse. Did you find anything?"

"Not yet. I ran everything you hadn't tested. Chemical reaction with basic viral agents and systematic reaction with antibacterial agents. Nothing obvious, but a few minor indicators. I'm just running them through the computer now. Anything new there?"

"No," DJ replied, with a grimace. "Still getting worse, not much else to say."

"Well, we'll keep working until we find it."

"Thanks, Doc."

He gave Doc a weak smile and cut the connection.

Doc sat back and wondered if he had missed anything. His thoughts were interrupted when his phone rang. He didn't recognize the number.

"Hello?"

"Hey, Doc, This is George Dewalt."

The voice sounded older. Doc didn't recognize the name.

"Uhuh?"

"With the train club. Down at the Mall?"

Doc vaguely remembered an old fellow with a limp that had just moved into the old folks home and had joined the club to keep busy. He'd been a railroader for years in the town where he used to live.

"Oh, George!" said Doc. "Sorry, I'm not sure that I ever heard your last name before. What can I do for you?"

"Well, the boys said I shouldn't bother you, but we're having a bit of trouble keeping that train of yours running and I thought maybe you could help?"

"I can try. What's happening?"

"Well, it's running out of juice before the day's out, almost every day. We're charging it like you said, but it doesn't seem to be lasting."

"I see."

Doc thought for a minute.

"You know, George, I'm at work right now. I've got to run a few tests, but they'll take a bit of time. Let me get them started and I'll pop down and have a look."

"That would be great," said George, sounding a little surprised. "Thanks!"

"See you soon."

Before he hung up the phone, Doc heard George talking to someone else.

"He's coming by to have a look."

"What? No way," said another voice.

There was a click and the call ended.

Wow, Doc thought, have I been that bad?

CHAPTER 25

At The Mall

When he'd first dropped the trailer with his riding train at the mall, Doc had popped inside to have a quick look at where they were planning to set up the train. Their plan was to have it run around Santa's village and have a railroad crossing where the people would cross to see Santa. It had initially seemed like that would work but Doc had suggested that they maybe have two crossings, one in and one out, for safety's sake. At that time they had already started to build Santa's village and had added just a couple of garlands to see how they were going to look.

This time when Doc arrived at the mall it looked as if the garlands had been infused with magic and grown out of control. They now covered almost every surface that he could see, escaping Santa's village and winding down the railings and posts of the mall. It truly looked like a Christmas wonderland.

As he walked up to the display, he saw a train running past and thought that he could already see part of the problem. The riding cars had been decorated with incandescent Christmas lights. They looked great, but Doc suspected that the power draw from the lights would be too much for the train's batteries.

Two of his old friends were running the train. Ken was driving with Harry seated on the back as conductor. Doc started over to say hello but an older man with a cane waved at him to come over behind the station and into a curtained off area set up behind the display.

"You must be Doctor Stevens," said the man, as he pushed the curtain open for Doc with his cane. "I'm George, thanks for coming down."

"Call me Doc. No problem, glad to help."

He looked around. There was a small table and chairs, along with a place for their equipment.

"This is nice. They never gave us an area like this before."

"George's doing," said Janice, as she came up from behind him.

"Hi Doc."

"Janice."

She was brief and to the point as always.

"George is the one who's been getting things organized these days. I'm guessing he called you?"

"I did, Janice, thank you," said George.

Doc greeted the three other club members seated at the table.

"Ross, Charlie, Arlene. Good to see you all."

They nodded to him as George continued.

"Really appreciate you coming down here, Doc, and for the loan of the train, but it doesn't seem to have enough power in the batteries. They're running out before closing time every day."

"I think the main culprit might be the Christmas lights on the riding cars," Doc began. "The battery was never designed to power incandescent lights as well as the motors. Can you bring it in so I can run some load tests on it? It'll just take a few minutes."

"Sure can," said George,

He nodded to Janice, who headed out to ask the others to bring the train in.

Doc grabbed a coffee and chatted with everyone at the table while Janice talked to the people waiting in line and put out signs that read 'Back in 10 minutes'. Ken and Harry soon ran the train into the back area. Doc's longtime friends were quite happy to see him.

"It's really good to see you out, mate," said Harry. "It's been a long time."

"I'm glad I came down," Doc replied. "It's going well?"

"Except for your darn train dying," said Ken, with a chuckle. "What are you doing down here anyway?"

Doc held up his hands in mock surrender.

"Hey, I'm just here to fix the train."

"Don't mind him," Harry said. "He's just mad 'cause he bet me a fiver you wouldn't show."

"Did not."

"Pay up!"

"Guys," said Doc, laughing at them. "Let's have a look at this train. Where's the multi-meter?"

Doc disconnected the lights, put the meter on the train and powered it up. He then reconnected the lights and tested them by themselves before conducting a final test with both running.

"Well, there you have it. It's the lights."

"Too much power?" asked George.

"Yes," Doc replied. "These are low voltage incandescents. Little lights but with a big power draw."

"They certainly are a big draw," said Janice. "With the lights on the train we've been busier than ever this year."

"What can we do?" Ken asked.

"A few things come to mind," replied Doc. "Turn the lights off or maybe only run them sometimes."

Judging from the negative looks he got from everyone, Doc realized that this was probably a bad idea. They must be doing really well, which meant that the current years' charity would raise lots of money.

"You could park the train for an hour at lunch and connect it to the charger," he suggested.

"Same problem," said George. "Downtime isn't good."

Doc thought for a moment.

"I can think of two other things that could do it, but they are both a bit of work."

"Well?" Harry asked.

"First, you could add a second battery from the lights and charge it separately. Or, and this might be the best idea, switch to LED lighting instead of incandescent."

"There's enough power for that?" asked Ken.

"Definitely." Doc said. "Lee Valley has some color LED strips that could do it for this year. Next year we could get RGB strips and write a program for twinkling lights and things."

"Will that mean you'll be around a bit more?" asked Janice.

"That would be really helpful," George added.

"I may be," said Doc. "I do have this one project that I have to get done first."

Janice simply rolled her eyes. She'd heard Doc's excuses before.

"Well, that's just fine," said Harry. "You get it done and then come on down here and run your train for a while."

"Actually," said Ken, pointing at the waiting lineup. "You're here now, so why don't you take a couple of loads around."

"I just can't right now. I have tests finishing at the lab and a big problem that I have to deal with."

Doc could tell that they were all thinking he was just blowing them off again. He couldn't blame them. He had spent three years pushing them away, after all.

"George?" Doc asked. "You'll look after getting the LED lights?"

"I will."

"And we'll get them installed," said Ken, as Harry nodded.

"Let me know how it goes," Doc remarked, as he backed out of the curtain.

He quickly walked away from his friends. He really needed to get back to the lab.

Doc Christmas and The Magic of Trains

CHAPTER 26

Jeanette Helps

Doc had to admit that he was stumped. He'd eventually gone home and had a good night's rest. He'd returned to the lab early and had since tested everything he knew against this germ. Nothing had changed. The computer had analyzed the results and come up with the same thing. Nothing.

He pulled up the image of the bacteria again. The centrifuge had not been able to separate the small and the large particles so the small ones were still in the picture. That bothered him. Doc had originally thought they might be a virus, but they hadn't attacked any host cells or the bacteria.

He was startled by a knock on his door. He wasn't expecting anyone.

"Come in?" he called.

Vicki pushed open the door and let Jeanette in first.

"Lunch is served!" said Jeanette.

"Sandwiches and soup," Vicki added.

"Smells good!" said Doc, who hadn't eaten since breakfast.

"Split pea and ham," said Vicki, as she placed the bowl on the table. "How's it going?"

"Frankly, not so well."

"What's the problem, Grandpa?" Jeanette asked.

Doc didn't know how to even begin.

"Well, that's a bit difficult to explain sweetie."

"Is this the problem?" said Jeanette, pointing at the image on Doc's monitor.

"Yes."

"It looks icky."

"It is icky," said Doc smiling. "We think this is what's making all the elves sick, but I can't find out for sure."

"Why not?" Jeanette asked.

Vicki winked at Doc, she was clearly enjoying the exchange.

"Yeah, Why not Dad?"

"Okay," Doc replied, with a sigh. "These big guys here are bacteria. There are good ones and bad ones in all of us, but these look a lot like the ones that give us pneumonia. That's like a really bad cold."

"Oh," said Jeanette as she stared intently at the screen.

"Anyway, I can usually run tests to see what things make the bad bacteria get sick. However, this time none of my tests are working so it's hard to find out what's wrong."

"Oh," Jeanette repeated, but she didn't sound as if she really understood.

"It's like if I show these big guys a picture and I ask them if they like it. They're supposed to say yes or no but they aren't saying anything."

"Hmm," said Jeanette, then pointed at the smaller particles.

"What are these little things?"

"I don't know," Doc admitted. "At first I thought they were a virus and maybe the problem. A virus is like a really small really bad bacteria. But these are the wrong shape and size for a virus and they aren't behaving like one either."

"How does a virus behave?" Jeanette asked.

He was about to cut off that line of questioning when Vicki spoke up.

"Thanks for being so patient with her."

Doc took a deep breath wondering how best to explain these things to Jeanette.

"A virus usually attacks cells, like the bacteria, and takes them over to make more viruses."

"That's not nice!" said Jeanette, sounding shocked.

"Viruses aren't nice. But these things aren't doing that so I don't think it's the problem."

"Maybe they can't hear you?" said Jeanette.

"What?"

"Maybe the big ones can't hear you when you ask," Vicki explained for Jeanette.

Doc looked at her, then back at Jeanette.

"Maybe there's too many small ones," Jeanette began, "and they're...

"In the way!"Doc exclaimed. "That could be what's happening! These could be inhibitors."

Jeanette looked confused.

"There might be too many of these little guys in the way. So they could be inhibiting the big ones from hearing me."

"For real?" Jeanette asked.

"For real," Doc replied, giving her a big hug. "I'm very glad you came by. I know what to do next."

He should have expected her next question.

"What?" asked Jeanette.

"Well," laughed Doc, "first I'm going to go back over all my tests and see if any of them were able to affect, or rather, talk to the inhibitors. And then we'll see."

Doc stood up.

"Thank Helga for the soup. I'll see you two later," he said, as he gently ushered them towards the door. "I have lots more work to do now."

He headed back into the lab with a renewed sense of purpose. He thought it was amazing that it had come from Jeanette, but then remembered that many things were clearer through the eyes of a child. He racked up all the slides he'd finished and started going through them again, looking this time, for an effect on the particles he was now sure were inhibitors.

CHAPTER 27

Back To The Pole

It took Doc the rest of the day, but he was finally able to at least identify that he was definitely dealing with an inhibitor. Although it was frustrating to go through all this work just to get through to the bacteria that was causing the problem, he knew it was the only way he'd ever determine the real problem. He was going to need some more sample material and he had enough data to report in, so he called DJ on the elfPad.

"Hello?"

DJ looked even worse than before and his voice was becoming hoarse.

"Hi, DJ. I have news."

"Good news, I hope?"

"Some, I think," said Doc. "I think there is an inhibitor at work here. None of my tests worked out because of the inhibitor. I'm guessing the same thing happened at your end."

DJ appeared confused.

"That would explain no results, but how would an inhibitor get in our systems. Maybe you have a bad sample?"

"No, it's in every sample. Remember the small particles that we couldn't identify? That's the inhibitor."

"Where would that come from?"

"I was hoping you could tell me, but it sounds like maybe not," said Doc.

"Do you know what it is?" asked DJ.

"Not yet," Doc admitted. "I'm trying to identify that now, so we can get through to the bacteria. I'm going to need more samples though."

DJ smiled, sadly.

"Well come get them. We don't exactly have a shortage."

Doc heard someone calling DJ in the background.

"I've got to go," said DJ

"Wait!" Doc exclaimed. "Uh, how do I get there?"

"Just get in the train and think of the destination. The system will bring you in."

DJ broke the connection and was gone.

"Just get in the train." Doc said to himself.

He pulled out Nick's briefcase, set it on the counter, opened it carefully and looked at the train. He closed his eyes and concentrated on the North Pole. He opened one eye, he was still in his lab. He pulled the briefcase over so it was in right front of him. He sat down and stared intently into the briefcase, focusing on the train. Nothing happened.

He pushed the briefcase away slightly. He looked around and saw his sample case. He would need that. He got up, retrieved it and slung it over his shoulder. Now he was ready. He went back to the briefcase and tried again. Whether he was standing up or sitting down nothing seemed to be working.

He tried to reconnect with DJ on the elfPad, but there was no answer so Doc left a message explaining his predicament. He didn't want to call the girls. He needed to figure this out by himself. He sat at his desk again and cleared his mind. He thought of trains. He also thought of Jeanette and Vicki's visit and how such an unwelcome disruption to his routine had returned him to a much happier place. He even thought of Marilee and for the first time in a long time, it didn't hurt. He felt sad, but the sadness didn't consume him as it had in the past. He was at peace with everything. Yet he still failed to shrink.

Frustrated, he realized that it wasn't going to work. Whatever special ingredient Nick had brought to Doc's magic travel equation was now missing. Doc knew that he was simply going to have to wait until someone came and collected him.

While he was waiting, he took a closer look at the briefcase layout. It was more than just a train set. The terminus for the train was a tiny city, but the tracks ran through hills, across a river, and through a tunnel underneath a 'lookout mountain'. When the track emerged from the mountain it curved across a viaduct that crossed the city's harbor. Everything was landscaped and most of it looked handcrafted. The trains seemed to stick to the tracks, and Doc figured out that the wheels themselves must be magnetic.

He noticed that one of the viaduct piers was tilted over and the track was slightly uneven at that point. He grabbed a scalpel, took out the blade, and used the tip to push it back into place. In a moment of deja-vu he remembered a very similar problem on his layout. Marilee had been helping, prying up on the track so that he could adjust one of the piers. When it had clicked into place, her smile had been priceless. In that moment of happy memory, the pier in the briefase clicked back into place and he smiled to himself... before shrinking to just the right size to get on the train.

He looked around and shook his head, then smiled again and climbed up into the train car.

CHAPTER 28

Things Are Not Good

As DJ had promised, the system had brought him in just fine. A tired and haggard Fetna had ferried him from the Hub over to the lab at the hospital, wished them well and taken off. Fetna told Doc that Nick was busy helping out with some essential services but would come by later to see how they were doing.

Doc was pretty sure that he could now do everything he needed from the hospital lab so he called Vicki to let her know he would be staying.

"I'll be up here for while. Maybe a day or so."

"Is there anything we can do?" Vicki asked.

"Not right now," replied Doc, "I'll keep in touch."

"Bye, Grandpa."

"Bye, Jeanette. See you both soon."

"Bye, Dad," said Vicki, as he hung up.

* * *

For almost 24 hours Doc and DJ tested and tried, examined and correlated, studied and then tried again, all to no avail. They simply could not identify or affect the inhibitor in any way. Every known test failed to yield its identity. Both Doc and DJ were dead on their feet by the time Nick finally arrived to check in.

Nick looked DJ up and down and immediately took charge.

"I prescribe rest for you."

Nick beckoned a couple of the healthier looking elf doctors over.

"Please make sure that he gets some rest, and whatever else you can do to slow his infection down."

They both nodded and DJ didn't protest at all. He smiled encouragingly at Doc and Nick as he let his compatriots lead him away.

"You look almost as bad," said Nick.

Doc just sighed, feeling defeated.

"Come with me," said Nick.

He escorted Doc from the hospital to the flitter waiting outside.

"It's about time you took a break," Nick said, as they climbed aboard. "You can't work all the time."

"So where are we going?" Doc asked.

"I thought maybe a quick tour," replied Nick.

"A tour?" Doc asked. "Now? Are you serious?"

"A change is as good as a rest, or so they say," said Nick, smiling at him. "You should see what it is that you're trying to save."

Doc shrugged.

"Makes sense."

* * *

Nick took them up to a high cruising altitude and hovered. Doc still thought that it looked like a model train set below them, even though he knew better now.

"You've seen the highlands," said Nick, gesturing to the mountains where the arrival platform was located. "But the land here is as varied as the world above. The City, Hub and Workshops are here in the midlands. Elves can live in whatever climates they choose, from the wintry climate that Fetna seems to like so much, down to the seashore and everywhere in between."

He tilted the flitter and headed towards the seashore.

"How long have you, er, they lived here?" Doc asked.

"As long as anyone can remember," replied Nick. "There are no records of when things began here."

He pointed at the sky.

"The physics are what you would might expect, luminescent algae, a large body of water, altitude variation, volcanic heat, indigenous plant growth. Everything you need for a self-contained microclimate."

"So to speak?" said Doc, laughing.

"So to speak," Nick agreed. "And don't ask about the size thing either. Nobody knows."

"Really?" said Doc.

"Do you ever think about why you're the height that you are?" Nick asked.

"Well, right now yes, but normally, no."

"Neither do they," said Nick.

The seashore was beautiful, with long rolling beaches and small homes lining parts of the shore and small communities laid out behind them. Piers old and new extended from the shoreline and boats in a variety of sizes were tied up at marinas. A large industrial pier was crowded with barges and ships all around. Rail lines led from the pier into the city, but none of the boats or trains were moving. Everything was quiet.

"There is some mining on the islands on the far side of the ocean," Nick explained. "But with the outbreak, everything has been recalled to port. All but the automated rail lines have been shut down after the train incident. The lines that are open are just to take people to the city."

From the sea they headed inland. Nick took Doc on a different route than the one that he'd taken with Vicki.

"What's that?" asked Doc, pointing ahead of them.

"Inspiration Mountain," Nick replied, as he adjusted the flitter's course. "You might want to see this."

* * *

Inspiration Mountain looked like a large rock had fallen from the side of the cavern and crashed into the valley below. As they drew closer, Doc saw a monument and pathways that led around the giant rock and seemed to go underneath it. Nick landed near the monument.

"This is an important monument to the elves," he explained, as they got out. "It's their monument to working together."

Doc could see now that the entire rock, which really did look the size of a mountain from below, was suspended about thirty feet above the ground. Yet he couldn't see anything actually holding it up. Nick smiled at Doc as he began telling him the story.

"The house underneath the rock used to belong to an elf who thought that he should be in charge of Elf-Tec. He was a brilliant elf and was responsible for a lot of forward thinking inventions. He just didn't like the idea of a group running Elf-Tec, he thought he could do a much better job alone. The story goes that he wanted to build his house right here under 'The Rock', as it was called before it fell, and he'd dreamed up an idea for a force field that would protect the house in case the rock fell. He built the device, and had one of the other members of the Elf-Tec group build the power supply for him. Just before they turned on the force field, he discovered that the power supply had not been built to his specifications, and that the other elf had changed the design. He wanted to change it back, but since it was already installed, they went ahead and powered up the field.

Not too long after he and his family moved in to their new home, 'The Rock' broke free of the cavern wall and collapsed down toward the house. The force field barely held, but lasted just long enough for him and his family to get to safety, shorty after which the field failed and his house was flattened.

Later, while trying to find out why things had failed, he found that the only reason he and his family were still alive, was the altered power supply. The other elf had built in a booster backup just in case. Humbled, he thanked the other elf and together they worked to build a field generator that would lift the mountain and truly hold it in place. The house was rebuilt as a museum and the mountain remains suspended today as a monument to working together."

"Wow," said Doc. "Quite a story."

"Would you like to go inside?" Nick asked.

"Maybe another time?"

"On with the tour then."

Back in the air, Doc was starting to look tired again.

"Maybe some cocoa with Fetna?" Nick suggested.

"That might be good," said Doc nodding.

Nick turned and headed towards the platform. Doc looked down as they passed over towns, schools, playing fields, factories, farms, and houses. They're just like us, he thought to himself. I have to save them.

CHAPTER 29

A Clue

The air was cool and crisp as Nick pulled the flitter neatly into the garage and parked next to what looked like it's identical twin. He and Doc climbed out and walked around to the coffee bar. Fetna was there already and he pulled a steaming hot Cocoa 47 for Doc, which he passed on to Nick.

"Maybe you can show me how you do that?" said Doc.

"Sure," Fetna replied. "There's an App for that."

"You're kidding right?"

"Not at all. Where is your elfPad?"

Doc pulled out the device, turned it on and flipped through a few screens. Sure enough there was a 'Cocoa' App.

"There's a list of types," Fetna explained. "Scroll down and select Cocoa 47."

"Okay," said.

"Now press 'Eject' and be ready to grab the handle."

Doc pressed the button. The surface of the elfPad shimmered and Doc could feel an odd buzzing in the air in front of it. A 3D wireframe drawing of a mug appeared on the screen then solidified. The picture spun around until the handle faced toward him, then it started to slide forward, getting closer to the screen. The handle started to materialize on the surface as they picture slowly continued towards him.

"When the handle is fully out, it'll pause," Fetna told him. "Just pull gently and not too fast, and your cocoa will be ready."

"Amazing," said Doc, in awe as he pulled the steaming hot cocoa from the elfPad. "Just amazing."

"It's one of the coolest things to come out of Elf-Tec in the last few years," Nick agreed.

"Working together?" said Doc.

"That's right!" Fetna exclaimed. "You saw our mountain?"

"I did," replied Doc. "It's beginning to make sense to me."

Fetna smiled and they each had a big sip of their cocoa. Doc was warmed, relaxed and focused by the healing drink and it made him look at Fetna in a whole new light.

"Fetna," said Doc, thoughtfully. "You're not sick."

"Um, maybe. I guess not," Fetna replied, with a shrug. "I haven't really thought about it. I feel fine."

"You are an elf, right?" Doc asked, "No offense."

"Yes, of course, and none taken."

Fetna looked at Nick.

"Why am I not sick?"

"I don't know," Nick replied.

"This is great," said Doc.

"What? Why?" Fetna asked.

"Because you're quite possibly the key to a cure," said Doc. "If every elf is sick except you, then you have an immunity or a resistance to the bacteria. If we can find it and replicate it, then we can cure everybody.

"So what do we do?" Fetna asked.

"We'll need to get you to the lab and run some tests," replied Doc. "But let's cover a few things first. "What's different about you compared to every other elf?"

Nick sighed.

"That's a big list."

"Ouch," said Fetna, with a smile. "That hurts."

Nick counted on his fingers as he presented the facts.

"Health nut, adrenaline junkie, likes heights, loner. What am I missing?"

Fetna smiled.

"Inventor of Cocoa 47, explorer of the real world and I also quite like cold weather.

"Whoa," Doc groaned. "Any one of those could be a factor."

"Really?" said Fetna.

"Really," Doc replied. "Talk me through a typical day for you."

"Well," he said. "I start with rounds. I go up to the surface to make sure that there's been no weather damage to the hut and I chip a piece of ice off the glacier and bring it back down with me."

"You go outside every day?" Doc asked.

"Where else would I get ice?"

Nick pointed at the mountains below them.

"Oh, that's different," Fetna explained. "The ice upstairs really is glacier fresh. Want to try some?"

"Not right now, but we'll bring some along," said Doc. "We have to consider everything."

Fetna continued to describe the rest of his daily routine. While it was an interesting and exhausting list, everything other than the ice water that he'd mentioned was either physical or psychological and would have to be tested for at the lab.

"Well, let's get going then," said Nick. "We've got a lot to do."

Fetna grabbled a bottle of his special glacier water and they walked around to the garage. He headed for the second flitter.

"I'll take this one," he said. "With everyone else sick there's a million things to do to keep this place running."

"Absolutely," Nick agreed.

"We'll get you back out there as soon as we can," Doc promised.

Fetna floated his flitter over the edge and then dropped it in a fall again, just as he'd done before.

"Maybe he scared the Virus away," Doc joked as Nick floated them out.

"Maybe," Nick said, smiling as he dropped their flitter like a stone, copying Fetna's daredevil maneuver exactly.

* * *

They landed at the hospital and Doc began a battery of tests. DJ was hobbled by his illness but helped out as best he could. As soon as they had what they needed from Fetna, both he and Nick headed out on what they described as 'errands'.

"What kind of errands?" asked Doc.

Nick replied matter-of-factly.

"Making sure the generating station is operating, the water treatment plant is running, checking the automatic trans-portation systems, that kind of stuff."

"All the stuff that's usually done by a bunch of people," said Fetna.

Doc didn't know what to say. These two were trying to keep the whole North Pole running by themselves.

"Good luck," he said, as they left.

Now that they had a direction in which to look, Doc and DJ learned fairly quickly that the water was indeed the delivery vehicle. Fetna's glacier water really was glacier fresh with no problems, but all the other water at the North Pole was permeated, not with the bacteria, but with the inhibitor! It became even more complicated when the tests on Fetna's samples showed that even he had miniscule levels of both the bacteria and the inhibitor in his system.

Through all the testing, DJ was not doing well. If there had been anyone else to help, Doc would have had him confined to bed a long time ago. However there wasn't another elf that was qualified and DJ had insisted on staying and helping anyway. They were completing the last test series on Fetna's samples when DJ slumped forward in his chair. Doc grabbed him and a couple of the remaining doctors helped lift him up onto a gurney.

"Doc," he said, weakly.

"Yes?"

"Fetna was sick. But it was a few years ago."

"I'll check it out," said Doc, but DJ had passed out and couldn't hear him.

CHAPTER 30

The Source

"Hi, Doc. Hey!"

Fetna grimaced. Doc had swung round and abruptly sat him down almost as soon as he walked through the door.

"Sorry. I need to take some more blood."

"What's going on?" Nick asked as he came through the doors. "Where's DJ?"

"He's down for the count," Doc replied." And Fetna here was sick a few years ago, with similar symptoms to what everyone has now."

"Hey that's right!" said Fetna. "I forgot about that."

"Well, DJ didn't," said Doc, as he pulled the syringe from Fetna's arm. "It was the last thing he said before he passed out. He keeps really good notes, which said that you got over it on your own?"

"That's right," Nick agreed. "I remember. You were

down for a couple of weeks. So, does that help us?"

"Maybe. If we are really lucky, Fetna may have developed antibodies to fight this off. If they are still in his system a solution may be at hand."

"That's great!" said Fetna.

"Not really. We also identified the source of the inhibitor, or at least the delivery mechanism. It's in the water. All the water. Except for your glacier water."

"But all our water is glacier water," said Nick. "As far as I know even our ocean is from glacier melt."

"You said it's in the water, Doc?" Fetna asked.

"Yes."

"But we have a filtration plant. Like Nick said, all the drinking water comes from a spring that's glacier fed and filtered."

Doc shook his head.

"There's no way you could filter this stuff. It's way too small."

"Too small?" said Fetna, not understanding.

"I'll show you."

Doc spun around in his chair and pulled up the live electron scan of the current slide. The automated system labelled tags for both the bacteria and the inhibitors. Before Doc could explain further he was interrupted.

"What's that?" Fetna asked, he was pointing at the tag on the screen that said 'Inhibitor'.

"That," Doc said, carefully, "is the problem."

"I've seen that word," Fetna was worried. He looked at them both. "I think I might know where this is coming from."

* * *

At Doc's suggestion, they donned environmental suits before they headed to the Hub. They flashed from the Hub to the train car in the quonset high above them. Fetna led them off the darkened platform and around the train car with the aid of flashlights. There were several stacks of aging 45 gallon drums in the back of the hut. Fetna led them to the farthest pile, beside the outside wall under the cliff face. The old labels were faded but the skull and crossbones poison sign could clearly be seen, as were the stenciled words, 'NERVE GAS INHIBITOR'.

"This could be it," said Doc. "But why would an inhibitor be poisonous?"

"And why now after sixty years?" Nick asked.

"These have been frozen a long time," said Fetna. "But about ten years ago, it started warming up and even thawing a bit in the summers."

He moved some junk around.

"Look here!"

They saw a small frozen pool of liquid under a rupture in one of the barrels. Fetna tapped the barrel with his flashlight. It sounded hollow and empty.

"Is that it?" Nick asked. "Could one barrel of poison do all this damage?"

Doc was still puzzled.

"Fetna, were there any pouches with documents or maybe a manifest of what's up here? Something that would tell us what this stuff is?"

"There's a binder on one of the other piles. Maybe that has something."

Fetna grabbed the binder and brought it back for Doc who quickly flipped through it. It was a safety manual. Inside were diagrams of how to survive the various types of attacks that an airbase might suffer during a war.

"Look!"

Doc pointed to an illustration of a soldier wearing a twin canister gas mask. The facing page was entitled 'Nerve

Gas Attack' and showed how to soak the the mask's pads in the inhibitor fluid to prevent the nerve gas from getting through. What Doc found most alarming were the DO NOT TOUCH and DO NOT INGEST warnings at the bottom of the page pertaining specifically to the inhibitor fluid.

"Good idea on the suits, Doc," Fetna said, nervously.

"We'll need a sample and anything we can get for identifying marks from those drums," said Doc.

'I'll help Fetna with that," Nick replied. "Maybe you should check the office for a manifest?"

Doc went into the old office and poked around. He found no manifest, or anything else that would help. But when he came back out, Nick and Fetna showed him a well-preserved label that read 'XT-127' on one of the drums. Maybe that would help them figure out what it was. Fetna chipped off a piece of the frozen fluid under the drum and they carefully sealed it in a jar from Doc's sample case. Then they quickly made their way back to the train car and flashed back into the Hub.

* * *

"XT-127 was an experimental nerve gas inhibitor created near the end of the Second World War to help troops survive a possible nerve gas attack," Nick read from the web. "Existence of the compound was confirmed after the passing of the Freedom of Information Act, and the subsequent declassification of many World War II documents."

Nick read the rest himself then summarized the information for the others.

"There's nothing here about what it was made from, how or by who. They do say there were no confirmed uses of either nerve gas or the inhibitor during the war and that all remaining stockpiles of both chemicals were destroyed."

"Not quite," Fetna said, sarcastically.

Doc put his head in his hands and thought out loud.

"So what do we know?"

"Everyone's sick," replied Fetna.

"Except you,"Doc reminded him. "We're dealing with an old, rare, manufactured bio-compound. It seems to affect the entire system, with the effect most discernible in certain bacteria at the cellular level. We know that Fetna's been sick with it before and that although he recovered on his own, he no longer has antibodies in his system. He does in fact carry the disease, as do all the elves at the moment.

"What else?" asked Nick.

"We can't yet identify the inhibitor, or the bacteria, although I'm not even sure the bacteria is involved any more. None of our tests have made a dent in the inhibitor's effect. It's as if it's inhibiting everything."

Doc looked up.

"Did I say that out loud? It's as if it inhibits everything."

"Yes, you've said it twice now," Fetna replied. "What does it mean?"

Doc had a look of triumph in his eyes.

"We have to inhibit the inhibitor!"

Doc Christmas and The Magic of Trains

CHAPTER 31

The Cure

For the first time since he'd heard about the epidemic, Doc felt that he might now know something that could be of value in combating it. When he arrived back at his lab, he immediately set up a culture series with a sample of the bacteria and inhibitors they'd collected from Fetna. He powered up the electron microscope then sat down at his desk and called home. There was no answer, so he tried Vicki's cel phone.

"Hi, Dad. Are you back?"

She was almost yelling, as if she was in a crowded area.

"Yes, I'm at the lab."

"How did it go?"

"A bit better, but there's something I could use a hand with that might help things. Can you come by?"

"Sure. We're at the mall but can be there soon."

"Great, thanks."

"Bye," said Vicki, as she ended the call.

Jeanette must be with her, thought Doc. Well, she could amuse herself while Vicki helped him with the test series. He went into the lab, checked the progress on the cultures then started preparing slides and equipment for a helper and another multitude of tests. When that was ready, he put a sample taken from Fetna on a slide and slid it into the electron microscope. He wanted one more look before he started.

* * *

When Vicki arrived he was at his office desk comparing two similar images and smiling. His smile faded slightly when Helga came through the door behind Jeanette.

That's why there was no answer at the house, he mused.

"Hi Jeanette, Vicki," Doc greeted them. "Helga."

Jeanette was happy to see him.

"Hi Grandpa. We went to see your riding train at the mall."

"Did you get a ride?"

"No, we had to come here," she replied, not sounding too disappointed.

Doc smiled at her.

"I'll take you for a ride when this is all over. Right now I could use everybody's help to see if we can cure this thing."

"Okay," said Vicki.

"What do you need us to do?" Helga asked.

"Let me bring you up to speed," Doc began. "We have a non-contagious epidemic in a contained environment and we haven't been able to identify the source."

He moved to the monitor on his desk.

"The top view is the infected sample, the bottom one is from the only person in the group who hasn't succumbed."

"There's less little ones Grandpa," said Jeanette.

"That's right. Thanks to Jeanette we started looking at the little ones, and it appears that they are a man-made inhibitor bacteria from a long time ago. I think that they are what's causing the problem. If I'm right, we should be able to use a phage treatment to fight them."

"Phage? You told me once that phage therapy can't be used yet," said Helga. "That it's not approved."

"That's true, it isn't approved for use here. We'll only be testing here and applying it elsewhere. Somewhere that it is allowed."

"Is it safe?" asked Vicki.

"I certainly believe so. It's been used for more than 60 years in Georgia and other Eastern European countries without serious incident."

He paused before continuing.

"Anyway, we first have to see if it'll even work and that's where I need your help. I have samples of hundreds of types of phage mixtures and I need to test them on this," he said, pointing first to the top image then to the one at the bottom, "to get to this."

"Let's get started," said Vicki.

They set up assembly lines in the lab and in the office. Jeanette stayed in the office and pre-labeled slides. Helga and Vicki donned safety gear and joined Doc in the lab. Vicki loaded slides with the infected sample and then Helga applied a tiny drop of each phage sample and passed it to Doc, who slid it into the microscope port.

"So what are you looking for?" asked Vicki.

"You see here the two bacteria, and these tiny things?" Doc explained. "Those are phages. I'm hoping to see one that has an immediate attraction to the bacteria. That will be a sign that it has the right protein marker."

"And then what?" asked Helga.

"Then, we'll see if it destroys the bacteria, lives inside it, or has no effect. This is going to take some time, and there is no way to know how long it will take. Once we've tested them all, then we'll go through and look at them again to see if there's a more delayed reaction."

Vicki was curious. "How do you even have these phage samples if they aren't approved?"

"I had a full series of bacteriophage cocktail samples brought in from Georgia to assist me in the detection and classification of rare diseases. I'm only allowed them for experimental uses and absolutely not allowed to use them on people."

The extra emphasis he put on the word people made Vicki look up. Doc smiled and winked at her.

* * *

Several hours later, they had finished the first pass of all the phages and took a break for something to eat. None of the samples had produced an immediate reaction. Doc was becoming worried that his phage idea might come to nothing, but he had to keep trying. They worked their way through the slides a second time. Nothing showed any effect until they got to sample number 149.

Doc had inserted the side and was rubbing his eyes. Helga looked at the monitor over his shoulder.

"What's that?" she said.

He looked up and focused in. The small bacteria were gone!

"This could be the one!" he exclaimed.

"Jeanette?" he called through the intercom before he noticed she was napping at his desk.

"I'll go," said Vicki.

She went through to the office and looked up the phage number for the test.

"T-92," she called to Doc.

Helga pulled phage mixture T-92 and Doc quickly set up half a dozen verification tests with it.

"Back to work," he said. 'We still have to get through the rest."

* * *

The rest seemed to take forever. Partly because they were waiting, partly because they knew something had already happened, and partly because Doc checked the six new samples every few minutes. Twenty-five minutes in, the six samples all showed the phages from mixture T-92 surrounding the smaller bacteria. They seemed completely uninterested in the larger organism.

"That's normal," Doc explained. "Phages are very specific. They usually only go after one target. We'll just watch these samples for a while and see what happens."

As they observed the slow motion drama, a cloud of phages surrounded the bacteria, some of them attaching themselves to the spots on the smaller bacteria, where they clung on for a while until they simply let go.

"This is the infection stage," Doc continued. "Where the phages infect the bad bacteria with their own DNA and hijack its system to replicate themselves. Then, they will either live inside the cell or replicate so much that they simply burst through the bacteria's walls. This part can take a while."

"How long was it last time?" Helga asked.

"Five to six hours," said Vicki, before Doc could answer.

She smiled at him and shrugged.

"What? I was paying attention."

Around five and a half hours later they saw the outer shell of the Bacteria deform and a small cloud of phages emerge from it. They checked the other five tests. One bacteria had been fully consumed, two looked as yet untouched and the last two were in the process of disgorging phages. Doc was very happy. He ushered everyone in to the office for a break.

"What next then?" asked Helga.

"Two things," said Doc.

He grabbed his elfPad and linked to Fetna.

"We're going to need to get some supplies brought in from Georgia, just in case."

"Okay," said Fetna, and immediately closed the connection.

"That was odd," said Doc.

"And the other thing?" Vicki asked.

"We need to test some samples from..."

None of them had noticed the soft glow coming from the briefcase train set. Fetna appeared directly in front of Helga, who promptly fainted. Fetna caught her and lowered her to floor gently.

"...Fetna," finished Doc.

* * *

They quickly briefed Fetna on the phage treatment and their progress. Once Helga awoke, they had to bring her up to speed on the whole North Pole situation. If she hadn't just seen Fetna appear from nowhere in front of her eyes, she might not have believed them at all. That didn't stop her from continuing to stare at Fetna in disbelief.

"So we'll need to go to the Elivia Institute in Tbilisi, Georgia and get enough T-92," said Doc. "I seem to remember there's a train service near there?"

Fetna was flicking through his elfPad at hyper speed.
"Got it."

He grabbed Doc's elbow. They glowed and were gone.

Helga was startled but leaned on the desk and steadied herself.

"I'm okay."

"They shouldn't be too long," said Vicki.

* * *

In fact Doc and Fetna were gone for almost an hour and then arrived back at the lab empty handed.

"What happened?" Vicki asked.

"Nothing," replied Fetna.

"We dropped the T-92 at the Pole before we came back," Doc explained. "Now we just need to test Fetna's samples with the T-92 and then, if he's willing, test him with a sample directly."

"That won't be necessary, Doc," said Fetna. "When you where explaining about T-92 earlier, I looked it up and found out that it could be taken orally."

"So?"

"While you were helping Helga come around, I took a sip of the sample vial."

Doc's jaw dropped.

"You did what? Why?"

"I figured you'd need to test it on one of us sooner or later. I'm the strongest one right now, so now you can test on me first."

"But Fetna," Vicki began.

"He's right." Doc interrupted her. "At some point it would have to be tested on an elf. So? How do you feel?"

"Same as always," Fetna replied, smiling.

161

"We'll see," said Doc.

Vicki, Helga and Jeanette waited in Doc's office while he examined Fetna.

"The phages are in your system and have started attacking the inhibitor bacteria. This could take longer because we're not dealing with an isolated sample on a slide but a whole system."

Fetna jumped off the examination table.

"Fine, then let's go."

"Not yet," said Doc. "We're not ready."

"No," said Fetna. "We're not, but if we wait until everything's ready it might be too late for some of us. Can't we get up there and get ready? We could pick some test cases there and get a... what do you call it? A baseline."

"That," said Doc slowly, "is a very good idea!"

"Vicki, Helga?" Doc startled them with the call over the intercom. "Can you wake Jeanette? We're going to head up to the Pole now and we'll need all hands on deck."

CHAPTER 32

Nick Says Thanks

They ended up spending the next two days at the North Pole, working tirelessly day and night to finalize the testing. Once positive reactions had been confirmed, Doc and the others helped Nick and Fetna make sure that everyone received treatment. Results were indeed promising. Those that had the mildest symptoms were already feeling well enough to help by the time Nick had sent them home to get some rest.

* * *

"Good morning," said Helga, to Doc as he came into the kitchen. "Have you heard anything?"

"Nothing yet," Doc replied. "I'll try after breakfast."

"Ah," said Helga, placing a nice hot cup of tea in front of him."Vicki said you prefer tea."

"Yes," said Doc with a smile. "Thank you."

Jeanette barreled into the kitchen for a hug.

"Grandpa!"

"Somebody had a good sleep," Doc said, as he hugged her back. "Good morning."

"Are we going to the North Pole today?"

"I really don't know."

"Don't know what?" asked Vicki, as she joined them in the kitchen.

"What's happening," Doc replied. "We'll check in and see how things are going after breakfast. Okay?"

"Sounds good," said Vicki.

Helga and Jeanette nodded their approval as well.

* * *

Helga had prepared a full breakfast of bacon and eggs, French toast, and even a fruit plate. After a day of rest and a good night's sleep, it was just what the doctor ordered. Just as they were finishing breakfast, there was a knock at the door.

"I'll get it!" cried Jeanette.

She ran for the door, with Vicki right behind her. They came back a minute later.

"There was nobody there," said Vicki.

There was another, louder knock at the door. They all looked at each other and realized it was coming from the door to the train room.

Doc stood up as Vicki went to the door and opened it. "Hello?"

An exhausted, but smiling Nick was standing at the top of the stairs.

"Come in!" said Vicki.

"Nick," Doc greeted him matter-of-factly.

"Doc," Nick replied, his smile growing wider.

"I hope you don't mind me just dropping in, but I don't get to do it very often. Well, not during the day anyway."

"Would you like some breakfast?" Helga asked.

"No thanks, Helga."

"How are the elves?" Jeanette asked.

"That's what I came to tell you," said Nick. "The elves are recovering quickly. DJ said to give you a message. He says 'Nicely done!'"

"And there are quite a few other people that want to say thanks to all of you."

"Well, what else can we do to help?" Vicki asked.

"To be honest, not very much," Nick said. "Many of the elves are already well enough to go back to work or help with those that were hit harder, but they're all responding well. And none too soon with Christmas only a week away."

"That's great news," said Doc smiling.

"I knew you could do it," Nick told him.

"Well, you couldn't know."

"With absolute certainty," Nick said. "You've done it before."

"What?" Vicki asked.

"I think I'd remember the North Pole," said Doc.

Nick took a deep breath.

"Not the North Pole. I knew you would remember the magic."

"I don't follow," said Doc.

"Do you remember when you saved that lady who fell off the train platform?" asked Nick.

"Of course."

"What do you remember?" Nick asked.

"She fainted," replied Doc. "I jumped down and pushed her off the tracks."

"Right before the train would have hit her," Vicki added. "Mom told us that story all the time."

"I suppose," said Doc. "People there said I threw myself flat between the tracks and the train ran over the top of me. I don't remember that part, just rolling out from under the train after it stopped. I was very lucky I didn't get hit."

"Yes, that's the part." Nick said. "Try and remember what really happened on the tracks."

"What do you mean?"

"Use what you now know to be true," said Nick, softly. "and try and remember a little more clearly."

Doc closed his eyes.

"I pushed her clear," he said. "I looked around but the train was almost on top of me."

Helga gasped.

"Then?" said Nick.

"I could see the coupler was coming straight at me. I..." Doc shivered.

"There's no way it could have missed me."

"So what happened?" Nick asked.

Nick smiled reassuringly at Jeanette, Vicki and Helga.

"I... The train. Glowed. Or maybe I glowed? I shrank down. I shrank!"

He opened his eyes.

"I shrank. How did you know?"

"The globe at the Hub senses those events," Nick replied with a smile. "We like to check into them."

Doc shook his head.

"You knew."

"And so did you!" said Nick, proudly. "Apparently without any help from us."

"I got bigger after the train had stopped, then rolled out from underneath." Doc said.

"Oh, Dad," said Vicki

She was in tears, followed shortly by Jeanette and even Helga.

"It was the first time anyone had done it completely on their own," Nick admitted.

"Wow, Grandpa,"said Jeanette. "You're famous!"

"And I," Nick added, standing up, "have to get back."

He pulled a small model engine from his pocket and set it on the table.

"I'll see you all very soon, and you of course, can drop in any time! This is not goodbye, I promise."

Nick was smothered in hugs. He gently pushed them away and smiling, he softly glowed. This time, Doc and the others witnessed the magic of him shrinking down until he was standing beside the train on the table. Nick hopped up on the steps into the cab. As he did the engine sprouted tiny miniature lights along it's length, becoming a Christmas train. He waved from the cab, glowed once again and was gone. The Christmas lights on the train slowly faded out.

Doc's elfPad chimed and startled everyone. Nick was calling them from the Hub.

"Oh, and if I don't see you before then, 'Merry Christmas'."

He winked and cut the connection.

Doc Christmas and The Magic of Trains

CHAPTER 33

Family Outing

It was still afternoon and the mall wasn't too busy yet. Doc held the door open for Vicki and Jeanette.

"After you, ladies."

"What are we doing here?" Vicki asked.

"I know!" cried Jeanette.

"And why is that, Jeanette?" Doc asked, with a big smile.

"For my train ride."

"That's right," he replied, before looking up at Vicki. "And maybe a little tree shopping later?"

"That would be nice," said Vicki.

Jeanette checked out store windows as they walked along through the mall, but Vicki seemed to be deep in thought.

"What's up?" Doc asked.

"All the excitement has thrown me off my plan to write

your biography. You know, for my final project."

"Why would it throw you off?"

"I was planning on opening with that story of how you saved the lady at the train station, but now... Well, I can't really tell the truth, can I?"

"I guess not."

"I'll need to rethink the whole thing."

Jeanette had spotted the trains and was already running in their direction. "C'mon!"

"Let's chat later?" he suggested, as they headed towards the display.

The train was gliding by as they arrived at the display. Janice was the engineer this time and she called to Doc as she passed by.

"Meet us at the station."

They walked over to the station and waited for the train to come in. Ross, who was now Conductor Ross, started clearing the train so that a new batch of riders could board.

"Right this way folks," he said.

He ushered them through the exit gate, then closed it and walked back along the train to let the next batch of passengers onto the platform.

Janice stopped him.

"Just a sec Ross."

She pointed out the new LED lighting to Doc.

"Well, what do you think?"

Before he could answer, Jeanette poked her head around Doc and into the middle of their conversation.

"Oh, hello there," said Janice smiling at her.

"Janice, this is my granddaughter, Jeanette, and I think you know my daughter?"

"Well, hello, Jeanette. Hi Vicki. What do you think of the new lights on the train?"

"Hi, Janice," said Vicki. "They're new?"

"Sure are." Janice confirmed. "We were having troubles with the other lights so Doc recommended the LED's."

"They're sparkly," said Jeanette.

"They sure are," Janice agreed. "Did you want to go for a ride?"

"Yes, please!"

"We should wait our turn," said Doc.

"Nonsense," Janice said, firmly. "It's your train! Just a sec."

She reached behind the counter and pulled out some lanyards with tags that read 'Member'. She then handed one to each of them.

"Janice, I really don't think..." Doc began.

But he'd forgotten that Janice wasn't the sort that took no for an answer. She turned and without warning introduced him to the whole line of people waiting for the train.

"Hi, Folks. This is Doctor Stevens, the fellow who donated his train so that you could all come for a ride today."

The crowd murmured appreciatively and a solitary 'Thank You' came from somewhere in the line.

"He and his family haven't ridden it yet this year," Janice continued loudly. "Would you mind if we let them join us on a trip around?"

Everyone in the line clapped and a couple of people cheered. There was no way Doc could refuse now. Janice seated them on the train before Ross opened the gate and filled the rest of the train up. Everyone made a point of saying thanks or shaking Doc's hand.

She smiled at Doc as she climbed onto the engineer's seat.

"Just thought you should know how much people appreciate this."

171

She gave a couple of toots of the train horn and the sound of a diesel engine powering up washed over them as they headed down the track.

Doc had to admit that they'd done a brilliant job of setting things up. The train went through Christmas-light covered arches, and a small forest of presents. The track provided a view of the rear of Santa's castle where a window allowed Santa to be seen from the train. Black cloths draped over the track were punctuated with cardboard tunnel portals to make them look authentic. They had even installed 'Railroad Crossing' signs with flashing red lights and bells for the places where the people crossed the tracks as they moved in and out of Santa's village. Doc admired the crossings even more, when Janice sounded the horn before arriving at the crossings and the red lights began flashing automatically.

* * *

After they'd gone around with two different train loads, Doc wanted to disembark at the station. Jeanette wanted to stay aboard, so Vicki remained on the train with her.

Janice had turned the engineer's job over to Marcel so she could chat with Doc.

"I didn't think we would see you until the teardown party," she said, then added. "Well, what do you think?"

She was obviously proud of what they'd created. Doc had no trouble praising their efforts.

"No wonder you're doing so well this year," he said. "The decorations, the length of the track, even the railroad crossings. It's all brilliant!"

"Thanks, Doc. That means a lot coming from you."

"How did you rig the crossings to light up?" he asked. "I didn't see a trip wire or a hand control?"

"That was Kevin's idea," she explained. "They work like real train signals and sense the oncoming train through resistance in the rails."

"Very nice!"

"Much of this is George's doing," Janice continued. "But it was pretty easy to get behind. When it's over, we will install the extra track we made for the mall display at the train track in the park. The signals will go there as well."

"And the decorations?"

"We've been building a collection for a few years. When's the last time you actually came to a Christmas mall run?"

"It was before Marilee passed," Doc admitted. "I've been away too long."

"Well, you're back now."

George had overheard the last part of their conversation as he came up behind them. "Hope you don't mind that we changed a few things."

Doc held out his hand and George shook it firmly.

"You've done a brilliant job," said Doc. "I'm glad my train still fits in the plan."

"You are still very much part of the plan," replied George. "We'll be seeing more of you?"

Doc watched Vicki and Jeanette waving at him as the train headed back towards the station. He looked at all the happy folks on the train and at his friends, old and new, happily pitching in to bring a bit of Christmas joy to others.

"I'm back," he said, simply.

"Excellent," said Janice. "Let's make this official."

George smiled as she grabbed Doc's arm and led him over to the station.

"You need to take it around a few times," she said.

Doc looked at Vicki and Jeanette, waiting hopefully on

the train, and at Maurice, who was holding up an engineers hat for him.

Doc smiled at his family, took the hat and put it on. He nodded to Ross at the back of the train and moved into the engineers seat. A casual observer might not have noticed that the train seemed to sprout a few extra Christmas lights when Doc sat down. But everyone could see Doc beaming back at Ross as he called out.

"All Aboard!"

He blew the horn, started the train and headed out from the station.

CHAPTER 34

Gotta Go Back

It was only a few days before Christmas. Doc's office door burst open and Jeanette rushed in, startling him.

"Mom can write a story about Nick!" she blurted out.

Vicki came in behind her.

"Sorry, Dad. She couldn't wait to tell you her idea."

"That's okay," said Doc. "What's your idea?"

Jeanette answered carefully.

"Mom says she can't write your biograp... biogra... your story now. So maybe she can write a story about Nick and the elves?"

"Whoa," he said, pausing for a moment. "I don't know. Can you write a story like that?"

"Well, sure," said Vicki, sounding slightly offended. "I could write it as a novel. A fictional story."

"Sorry. What I meant... Will it work for your final project?"

"Oh, I think so. Any written work should be acceptable."

"Hmm. It's an interesting idea," he said, then looked at Jeanette. "There's just one very important thing that needs to be done first."

"Ask," said Vicki.

"Ask," Doc agreed.

"Because it's a secret?" said Jeanette.

"Exactly," Vicki replied. "It's a secret that Nick and the elves might not want everyone to know."

Jeanette was heartbroken.

"Oh," She said.

"But," Doc reassured here, "we can definitely ask."

"Really?"

"Of course. What would happen if they wanted the story told, and we didn't ask?"

"I guess we won't know unless we do," agreed Vicki.

Doc smiled and pulled out his elfPad. He selected Nick and waited for him to answer, but there was no response.

"That's odd!"

He tried again, but there was still no reply.

"Maybe he's busy?" Vicki suggested. "Christmas is coming up fast."

"Perhaps. I'll try Fetna."

However, there was no response from him either. Doc then tried DJ. Then the main number that Nick had said would connect him to Cyril. There was no answer on any of the lines.

"Maybe it's broken?" said Jeanette.

Doc selected the Cocoa App and pulled himself a Cocoa 47.

"Seems to be okay."

"Maybe try later?" Vicki suggested.

* * *

They tried again a couple times over the next hour without success and they were starting to get worried.

"Well," said Doc, as he pulled Nick's train briefcase out from under his desk. "Let's go and have a look."

As a precaution, he grabbed a medical kit for himself and one for Vicki to carry. They all stood in front of the briefcase and a moment later were gone.

Doc Christmas and The Magic of Trains

CHAPTER 35

A Small Complication

The automated systems at the Hub had recognized the briefcase, reconfigured the transfer car and brought them in safely. Doc, Vicki and Jeanette climbed down from the train car. The platform was completely deserted. Curious and worried, they climbed the stairs to the main platform. The consoles were active and the globe shimmered brilliantly with multi-colored dots. There just wasn't anyone there to see it except them.

"This is really strange," said Vicki, voicing the concern they were all feeling.

A faint voice broke the silence from high above.

"Hello!"

A buzzing sound quickly grew louder as Fetna rappelled down from the upper rafters. In one continuous motion he un-hooked his cable, did a little flip, and landed on his feet in front of them.

"What's up, Doc?" he said with a straight face, then burst out laughing. "I always wanted to say that!"

"Where is everybody?" Doc asked.

"Well, the elves are still on the mend, but there seems to be a side effect to the cure. Apparently we elves are now infectious to non-elves".

Vicki pulled Jeanette back slightly, but Fetna calmed her fears.

"Don't worry, not me. I never really had it!"

Doc nodded.

"That's right," Fetna never had the symptoms and we've been around him all along. What about Nick?"

"Yes, Nick has become very sick too!"

"We tried to call," said Jeanette.

"Everybody's very busy now," Fetna explained. "If they're not helping with the sick, then they are busy catching up on production."

"Can we talk to DJ?" asked Doc.

"Sure."

Fetna went over to a console and tried DJ. When there was no answer, he called DJ through an intercom. Moments later DJ called back. He was still pale from the virus.

"Hello, Doc," He said.

"It's true?" asked Doc, and added. "How's Nick?"

"Yes," DJ replied. "I've adapted your phage treatment and he should be through the worst of it in about twelve hours."

"You're all contagious?"

"It certainly appears that way," said DJ. "The small bacteria are no longer the problem though. When they were eliminated, the larger bacteria, a relative of your Streptococcus bacteria, became active."

"So you're contagious with pneumonia?" Doc asked.

"Of a type, yes," replied DJ.

"But what about Christmas?" said Jeanette, alarmed.

Fetna shrugged helplessly.

"The presents are coming along. We're catching up from the virus. We should be ready, but we won't be able to deliver them."

Doc looked at him quizzically. Fetna tried to explain.

"We elves always help with the deliveries. Nick is only one man, after all. But there's no way we would risk infecting the kids of the world."

"I see," said Doc.

"It's just too close to Christmas to be safe," Fetna said, sighing.

"Can you link me to DJ again?" asked Doc.

The elfPad relayed Doc's words.

"Uh, I'm still here," said DJ.

"Good. Can you send me Nick's data and the formula that's working for him?"

"Of course. I'll send it over shortly."

"Thanks," said Doc, as the call ended. "Fetna, I think I have an idea. Can you keep making sure everything's ready? For delivery?"

Fetna nodded, smiling at Vicki and Jeanette.

"Let's go."

Doc headed towards the stairs that led down to the tracks below.

"We'll be back soon," He called to Fetna as they descended. He smiled as he helped Vicki and Jeanette up into the transfer car.

"Seems we have a bit more work to do."

Doc Christmas and The Magic of Trains

CHAPTER 36

Stepping Up The Game

It was getting late on the day before Christmas Eve, when Doc was finally ready. He called Vicki.

"Okay, I'm almost done."

"We'll be right there," she said. "Do we get any clues yet?"

"I told you. It'll be a surprise," replied Doc and hung up.

He loaded the last few syringes into a case full of one-shot doses. There were still half a dozen on the tray. He nodded to himself and closed the case then reached under his desk for Nick's train briefcase. Doc really had no idea if his plan was going to work. He just knew he had to try.

* * *

The girls arrived at the office a little later, accompanied by Helga.

"I'm glad you're here," said Doc, then asked Jeanette. "Did you have an extra big nap like I suggested." He asked Jeanette.

"I tried, Grandpa."

"She hasn't really napped in a couple of years." Vicki added.

"Okay. Well, we all need to be vaccinated. I'll go first."

"What's that mean?" Jeanette asked.

She then saw the needle that Doc had picked up. He smiled and then injected himself while he explained.

"This is a vaccination so that we won't get sick while we're helping the elves."

To Vicki's amazement, Jeanette looked Doc straight in the eye and bravely held out her arm. He continued explaining while he injected her.

"If we have this, it will also keep any other people we see from getting sick because of us."

Focused on what he was saying, Jeanette hadn't even noticed that he'd finished.

"It didn't even hurt, Mom," she said, cheerily. "You go next."

"Okay," Vicki said, holding out her arm for Doc.

"So what is the plan Doctor?" Helga asked, as she received her injection.

Doc smiled and slid the train briefcase in front of them.

"You'll see," he said, as he handed each of them a case of syringes. "Lets go."

They shrunk down and boarded the model train.

"I'm not sure exactly how this is going to work," Doc admitted. Everyone sit one seat behind the other in a straight line."

"Where are we going, Grandpa?" Jeanette asked, before she began glowing with the rest of them.

CHAPTER 37

Closing Down, Starting Up

Long ago, Doc had established a rule that the train club wouldn't run trains at the mall on Christmas Eve. This was so that they could spend Christmas Eve with their own families. Because of this, the annual tear-down party on the eve of Christmas Eve, had become the club's major social event of the year. The mall was happy to have them and let the club's members stay as long as they wanted.

Fortunately, things hadn't changed, and while Doc had been away, the tradition had grown. This year there were more than 60 people at the party. Their group included train members, their families and some of their friends who'd come along to help with the tear-down. Doc's riding train had been parked for the day, the batteries totally drained from the day's trips. It was therefore something of a surprise to everyone, when the crossing signal lights suddenly began flashing and the train's horn sounded. From behind the briefly glowing curtain, Doc drove his riding train around the bend and into the station.

"Yay!" Jeanette called out from the train.

Vicki smiled at her Dad.

"I hope this was part of your plan?"

"Now for step two," he said, winking at her and Helga. "I'll need everyone's help with this part though."

They were immediately inundated with questions from everyone.

"I thought that thing was dead."

"Where did you come from?"

"How did you sneak in?"

They managed to avoid the more unanswerable questions and focused instead on getting reacquainted with some of the people that they hadn't seen in a few years. After a while George, looking visibly worn down from the weeks spent organizing, leaned heavily on his cane and got up to speak.

"Another great year everyone. Thanks so much for all your assistance," he said. "And a special thanks to Doc Stevens, whom I've finally got to know a bit this year, and without whom all this wouldn't be possible."

There was loud clapping shortly overshadowed by Ken and Harry loudly calling out.

"Speech! Speech!"

Doc stood up and headed over to the microphone. He took a deep breath.

"It's been far too long," he began, speaking from the heart. "But I'm so glad to be here with my family, and my good friends."

He paused as he contemplated how to proceed.

"I've been away a lot since I lost Marilee. Thank you for helping me and my family feel welcome here again. In the past few weeks something really important has come up and now I, or rather, we need your help to fix something."

The room was silent and everyone was focused on Doc until Jeanette cried out.

"Fix Christmas!"

Everyone laughed at that and even Doc had a chuckle.

"I know It sounds crazy, but actually, she's right."

Everyone in the room was now looking at him as if he was crazy.

"Christmas is in trouble this year, but I think with your help we can fix it."

"What are you talking about?" George asked.

"Er, Doc?" said Janice, wanting to protect him from making a fool of himself.

Harry and Ken jumped up from their seats and came over.

"Are you alright, mate?" Harry asked.

"Cause you're talking crazy talk here," Ken added.

"I'm fine," said Doc, but he was getting frustrated.

"Dad!" Vicki called, to get his attention.

She handed him the elfPad. Fetna was on the screen, smiling and suggestively holding up a steaming mug of Cocoa 47. Doc smiled back and mouthed a silent 'Thank You' before resuming speaking to the audience.

"Look I realize this might be a bit much to take in," he said, as he activated the elfPad's Cocoa App. "Perhaps we can talk about it over a nice cup of cocoa? George, you look beat, why don't you have a cup?"

Trying to make sure everyone could see, Doc reached in to the elfPad screen, and pulled out a mug of steaming hot cocoa. He handed it to George, who had been standing leaning on his cane listening. When the cup appeared out of nowhere George was startled and sat down heavily, almost falling off the chair. He didn't look good.

187

Maurice, one of George's good friends intervened.

"That's enough, Doc. I don't know what you'd hoped to accomplish with that little magic trick but it's not funny."

Meanwhile, Jeanette had grabbed the cocoa from her grandpa and gone ahead and offered it to George anyway.

'Try some," she said.

Between Jeanette's innocent smile and his own curiosity George couldn't resist. He took a cautious sip. Everyone in the room was watching as he realized it wasn't bad. Then he took a huge gulp.

"Wow," he said as color flowed into his face. "What is in that?"

Energy seemed to flow into him. He looked at his legs and then stood up easily as people gasped. He had another gulp of the cocoa then set his cane down and strode straight up to Doc.

"Doc," George demanded. "What the heck is this stuff?"

Doc smiled. He certainly had their attention now.

"It's called Cocoa 47 and a new friend of mine makes it. Would anyone else like to try some? Maybe then you could hear the rest of what I have to say?"

* * *

A little while later, after everyone had tried some Cocoa 47 and was milling around talking, Janice whistled to get everyone's attention.

"So Doc," she said, once the room was quiet. "What's all this poppycock about Christmas?"

"Well, to start with, it's really important, and you my friends, are the perfect people for the task. You see, this is a train project of epic proportions."

CHAPTER 38

Doc Brings Them In

Nick's elfPad buzzed with an incoming call. Didn't they know he was still recuperating? Not that it would do any good the way things were going this year. He sighed and accepted the call from Fetna. From the background, it looked as if he was linking in from the Hub.

"If you're up for it, there's something you should see down here."

Fetna stepped out of the frame and showed Nick the scene behind him. Doc and a small crowd of were people disembarking from the transfer train, looking about in amazement.

"Isn't it great?" said Fetna, although his expression changed when he noticed Nick's look of disapproval.

"Please put Doc on," Nick said calmly.

Fetna handed Doc his elfPad, while gesturing to try and let him know that Nick was less than happy.

"Hi, Nick," said Doc.

"Hi, Doc. What are you up to?" Nick asked, politely.

"I have a plan, but I need to discuss it with you. I'll be right there."

"Doc!" Nick exclaimed, holding up the IV drip still attached to his arm. "Contagious, remember?"

"Ah," said Doc, smiling as he held up the case he was carrying. "Vaccinated!"

Nick shook his head.

"Get Fetna to bring you. And please keep those other people inside the Hub building."

* * *

When Doc arrived he discovered that, as Fetna had implied during their trip, Nick wasn't a very good patient. He definitely wasn't happy with Doc.

"What do you think you are doing bringing all those people up here?" he demanded, as Doc entered.

"Fetna told me what's happening," Doc replied. "I can't make the elves less contagious, but I've already vaccinated these people so that they can be around the elves and not be contagious to other people."

"So? What for?" Nick asked.

"To help deliver Christmas, of course," replied Doc. "Fetna told me the problem. These folks can be the solution."

"These people? Deliver Christmas? There's no way that can work"

Nick paused and then tried to explain.

"The elves always help with deliveries. They actually do most of them. But these untried, untested..."

"Train people," Doc interrupted him. "These friends of mine who are totally into both the magic of trains and the

190

magic of Christmas? These people who a couple of hours ago did not know the North Pole existed, yet were able to get on a model train and used their own beliefs to make it here on the first try, each and every one of them."

Nick listened attentively, but was obviously shocked. Nobody had really ever talked to him like this before.

"These people give up most of their own Christmas every year to help others celebrate the joy of the season," said Doc. "Nick, I know its a risk, but I trust these people, just as you trusted in me."

Nick said nothing, so Doc continued.

"Look, I don't even know what's involved with the whole delivery thing. But if it can be done, you have to let us try."

Nick reached over and linked to Fetna on the elfPad.

"They're vaccinated?" he asked Doc.

"Yes."

"Fetna, tell Cyril to get started on their training," said Nick, glancing at the clock on the wall. "You have less than 24 hours."

Nick closed the connection and looked at Doc.

"What are you waiting for? You have to get to training as well."

"Right! Bye!" said Doc and rushed for the door.

"Doc!" Nick called after him.

"Yes?"

"Good Luck!"

"Thanks."

CHAPTER 39

Training Time

Doc and Fetna arrived back at the Hub just as Cyril was getting everyone moved up from the train platforms below to around the consoles on the main level. Once everyone had assembled, he addressed the crowd.

"Okay people!" he began, sounding more like a drill sergeant than an elf! "My name is Cyril and my job is to train you to help deliver Christmas. I'm going to go over how this works so that you have a better understanding of what's needed, then we'll run a few drills. Let me tell you, this will be interesting, this will be magical and this will be fun!"

Jeanette waved her hand.

"Yes, Jeanette?"

"What will us kids do?"

"You'll be with a relative unless you and your parents decide you're okay to deliver on your own."

"But what..."

Cyril smiled at her kindly.

"Jeanette, a lot of your questions will be answered during training. Can it wait until then?"

"Yes."

"Right then," said Cyril as he turned to Fetna. "Sound General Quarters for the delivery teams."

Fetna nodded and touched a control on one of the consoles. A low pitched sound, reminiscent of a naval General Quarters rang out from outside the dome.

"Each of you will be working with a team of elves, who will be arriving shortly," Cyril continued, gesturing toward the globe. "Until then this is our guide. We deliver by sections, or time zones, as you call them."

Fetna was working the console and as Cyril spoke the globe went dark except for the outlines of the continents. A faint brightness indicated which sections were in daylight and which were in darkness. Time zone boundaries appeared around the globe, and the first one, GMT 0, was highlighted. Then the next ones were illuminated, one at a time until the highlight had moved right around the globe.

"As you may have guessed by your journey here," Cyril continued, "trains now play the major role in present distribution. Wherever there is both Christmas magic and the magic of trains, there is a portal that we can deliver through. The portals are indicated by a blue dot."

The globe shimmered blue as Fetna switched on the portal indicators.

"We use tourist railways, mainline passenger trains, model train layouts, and even old abandoned trains as way stations," said Cyril.

With each category he mentioned, a series of brighter blue dots appeared around the globe.

"We transfer trainloads of gifts from here at the Hub to those way station trains. Nick and we elves then deliver the presents to individual houses from each way station."

He paused for effect and smiled encouragingly.

"However, as Doc has told you, this year we elves will have to stay in the train and co-ordinate the operation. You new, er, helpers will be distributing the presents."

There were lots of murmurs from the crowd.

"Won't they see us?"

"How long will this take?"

"How do we know which presents go to which house?"

"People, people," said Fetna, calming everyone down. "We don't have a lot of time. Distribution and timing will be handled by the elves you're working with."

He gestured toward the teams of elves that had gathered behind them, and they stepped forward from the shadows, their earpieces flickering with excitement.

"It will be tight," Cyril continued, "but I believe that with your help, it should be possible to complete delivery on time. Fetna here will break you into groups and teams and you can continue your training with your teammates."

The Hub then descended into chaos as the elves surged forward to meet their new partners while Fetna and Cyril attempted to coordinate groups and teams. Eventually groups started to split off from the crowd and headed off in different directions.

* * *

Fetna stood before half a dozen mixed teams.

"Some of you asked 'what if they see you?' The answer is... Elf-Tec."

The elves in the team helped their human teammates

clip a small object to their belts. It resembled an electronic bug repellent device.

"When the cloak is turned on," Fetna continued, "this little beauty emits a modified pheromone mix that essentially causes anyone that spots you to see what they want to see. This does not affect the wearer."

The elves switched on the cloaks and the half dozen humans in the group each looked around at five other Santas.

"Fetna?" said George, raising his hand. "Why do I see five Santas standing here with us?"

"What?" Fetna replied in alarm. "Anyone else?"

All the Santas raised their hands, and noticed that they were each looking at their own gloved hands and red sleeved arms.

Fetna grabbed his elfPad and made a call.

"DJ? I think we're going to need a different pheromone mix for the new helpers."

* * *

"Go!" Cyril called to his group of teams on the platform. As everyone watched, the elf named Johnson hopped onto the train, his teammates waiting anxiously behind.

"ReCon."

They heard Johnson over the elf pad, and a small glow emanated from the train. A couple of minutes later the train car glowed again and the elfPad crackled.

"All clear!"

Cyril nodded to the rest of Johnson's team, and with the other teams watching, they hopped up into the train and squeezed past Johnson into the very few spaces between the many presents that were packed inside.

"Ready!" said Johnson, into his elfPad.

The train glowed from inside with a pulse that started at the front and went all the way to the back. Through the windows the other teams watched as the presents, Johnson and his team members all vanished from the train.

* * *

"Where are we?" Maurice asked.

They had reappeared inside a similarly configured, but totally different train. Lights shining in through the windows showed them that they definitely weren't in the same place anymore.

"We're now at the Canadian Railway Historical Museum," said Johnson. "It's one of our training facilities."

"They know you're here?" asked Maurice.

"Oh, no, but we know that there are a lot of unattended trains here. However, we always ReCon first, just in case."

Johnson spoke into his elfPad.

"Complete."

* * *

Moments later Johnson and his team arrived back at the Hub, complete with the presents. As the glow faded the team disembarked the train.

"So, what was that for?" Maurice asked. "We didn't do anything?"

Johnson smiled.

"No, but you didn't freak out and that's what the test was for. Even some elves can't handle traveling by magic, so we test everyone, just in case."

"Did any of our people fail? Maurice asked.

"Not yet."

Johnson winked and led his team off to the next training exercise.

* * *

Fetna and Cyril stood alone for a moment, observing over the sea of confusion.

"There's not going to be enough of them, is there?" said Fetna.

Cyril shook his head, sadly.

"I really don't think so. Twice as many might do it, but its hard to tell."

Helga had remained silent, quietly taking in everything going on around her during training. When she overheard what they were discussing she walked over to them.

"I might be able to help you with that."

CHAPTER 40

People Power

The train was moving when Helga and Fetna appeared in the converted baggage car. Inside, it looked like a cross between storeroom and a gift shop. A lurch of the train threw Helga against Fetna, who caught her and helped her find her balance. They paused a moment and looked into each others' eyes, but whatever was there would have to wait. Fetna cleared his throat and let her go.

"Are you sure about this?"

Helga simply smiled and grabbed a brochure from the counter and showed him.

"Look."

The brochure was entitled *Christmas Eve Supper on the Train, sponsored by the National Railroad Historical Association.*

"These are train people as well," Helga explained. "Just

as Doctor Stevens knows his people, so I know mine. Let's go."

The next car was the kitchen and the cooks and serving staff were in full preparation mode. Helga ignored their questions regarding how she and Fetna had ended up in the gift shop, and instead enquired politely about how long it would be until dinner was served. The headwaiter looked at them in annoyance, then at his watch.

"Dinner will be served in precisely 25 minutes," he said, politely. "It would be best if you returned to your seats and perhaps enjoyed a glass of wine before dinner."

Fetna nodded and escorted Helga through the kitchen into the vestibule.

"Or maybe a cocoa?" he whispered to her.

She smiled as they opened the door to the bar car.

"Helga!" the bartender greeted her, warmly. "I didn't know you were on this trip."

She smiled at him. "A last minute decision, Pierre," she replied smiling. "Do you think you could get everyone's attention for me?"

Pierre turned the music down then grabbed a wine glass and tapped it with a spoon.

"Hello! Everyone? Helga would like a moment."

A few people waved in greeting and soon everything was quiet.

"This is my friend Fetna," Helga began, "We would like to quickly tell you a story. Perhaps you would like a cup of very special cocoa while you listen?"

Fetna smiled and began pulling a cup of cocoa from the elfPad. While the shock of watching a Cocoa seemingly materialize from the screen was settling in, he handed the mug to the first person that appeared interested, then moved to the next.

"Some of you know I've been helping Doctor Stevens on and off for the last few years," Helga began. "But this Christmas, something very special has happened and now we need your help."

* * *

The headwaiter sighed as he entered the bar car. He never enjoyed having to usher people away from their drinks, but the trays of salad were almost ready in the kitchen behind him and it had to be done. The last thing he expected was to find the bar car empty. Even the bartender was gone, which was really odd. As he went through the car the headwaiter noticed half-full glasses remaining on many of the tables.

When he reached the next car and saw that it was empty too, he nervously retreated back into the bar car to get help. A couple of the waiters had followed him loaded with their salad trays, and he beckoned them to follow him. They set down their trays and together they looked curiously throughout the train. The first three cars were all empty. Everyone was gone!

As they entered the second last car, a fading glow could be seen through the vestibule door. The glow was coming from the observation car, the last car on the train. They ran, but when they arrived, the observation car was empty too, except for a solitary old man sitting at the very end of the car. He was sitting facing out the back window of the observation car, holding a cup of steaming hot cocoa in his hand.

The head waiter ran up and shouted questions at him. The old man simply looked up and cupped his ear. Realizing that the man must be deaf, the headwaiter shrugged in an animated attempt to ask where everyone had gone. The old man smiled and pulled out a pad and pen. He slowly and carefully wrote a note and passed it to the headwaiter.

"They had to make a quick stop. Will be back on Christmas Day".

The old man smiled again, perhaps at the consternation and confusion that his note had caused. As he stared out of the train's back window, he could easily have been reflecting on how nice it was, at times like this, to be deaf.

CHAPTER 41

The Process

Helga and Fetna flashed into the transfer car at the Hub with the last carload of passengers from the *Christmas Eve Excursion Train*.

"But why did we leave that man behind?" Fetna asked. "I don't understand."

Helga smiled at him.

"Don't worry, he wouldn't have been that much help here anyway, he's stone deaf. He will stay behind and let them know that we'll be back. So much better than everyone just disappearing, don't you think?"

"Yes, I suppose. But, how do you know we can trust him."

"Fetna," said Helga, softly. "He's my father."

They disembarked from the car and joined the rest of the new helpers for their introductory session and training.

* * *

It was some hours later before Fetna and Cyril had finished the last training sessions and were able to join the preparations for the first wave of distribution. The consoles were all manned. The globe had been adjusted for the best visibility with the starting line - the international dateline - displayed in front. Trains of all shapes and sizes had been queuing up for hours on the platforms below.

A tense, almost electric, feeling of anxiety had been slowly building up inside the hub ever since Doc had arrived with his batch of helpers. Suddenly, in the middle of the sea of frenzied, organized chaos, a calm slowly spread. Within moments the noise and the hubbub had died down to a whisper.

All eyes turned to watch Nick as he came to the front of the main platform. He still looked ill, but he wouldn't have missed this moment for anything.

"My friends," he said emotionally, then paused. "My friends. Those words have new meaning for me today. Doc? Where are you?"

Nick saw Doc wave from where he was standing with his team.

A cheer rang out from everyone in the building before Nick raised his hands for quiet.

"And all our new helpers?"

Another cheer, even louder swept through the building as all the new helpers slowly raised their hands.

"Indeed," said Nick, glancing at the globe, "we have so many new friends joining us today." My friends, our celebration will come later. Christmas is upon us. Your time is at hand."

Another cheer rang out and merged with a loud buzzer that echoed through the huge structure as the first time zone on the globe became illuminated. The globe's blue train portals flickered on the globe in that time zone as well as others all over the world. A multitude of other colored lights also lit up. From the platforms below, the teams could see parts of the globe through the grating to get a sense of what was happening.

Then, a single blue dot glowed brighter on the far northern end of Russia. An elf at one of the consoles spoke into his microphone. On the tracks below a single elf jumped onto a train and the compartment glowed. Moments later the train glowed again and the elf was back, ReCon completed. Janice's team hopped onto the train, the train glowed along it's length, and the presents and people it had contained moments before were gone. On the globe, the bright blue dot turned a brilliant orange. The train driver then whistled his intentions moments before the train slid out of the station, another moving smoothly into it's place.

Another blue dot on the globe flared into brightness, followed by several others. Teams were dispatched and the corresponding lights on the globe soon changed to orange. Around the first bright orange dot, tiny blue dots flickered, then turned orange, then green, then winked out. More and more portals became active and more teams were dispatched. A smooth, methodical rhythm took hold of the Hub.

Doc's team's turn was coming up and their team leader Alfonso had them ready to board their assigned train. Just before they boarded, Doc noticed a transfer car glowing. When it faded, Janice and her team hopped down from the car, received new instructions, and headed off to their next platform. Doc looked up at the globe above and thought he saw part of New Zealand. Even as he watched, a blue dot on that area of the globe suddenly became brighter.

"This is us!" Alfonso shouted. "ReCon go!"

Moments later they got the all clear, hopped aboard the train and crammed in among the full load of presents. Doc smiled to himself as he watched his companions glow brightly.

CHAPTER 42

Deliveries

The lighting coming in from outside their train changed from the reflections of the brightly illuminated platforms of the Hub to a few stark shafts of light sneaking in through the darkened rail yard. As the glow of their arrival faded, the only lights Doc and his team could see outside were a few bare bulbs hung on poles. The air had the faintest tinge of salt indicating that they probably weren't too far from the seashore. The elves powered up their elfPads and flicked on their earpiece lights, so that they could see the presents more clearly as they positioned themselves along the train car.

"We'll be ready in a moment," Alfonso told Doc.

"Where are we?" asked Doc.

"As long as you don't ask every time," Alfonso replied with a sigh.

He smiled and pointed at the top of his elfPad's screen.

"We're at the tourist railway 'Steam Incorporated', in Paekakariki"

"Oh," said Doc said. "And, uh, where is that exactly?"

"New Zealand. North Island. Anything else?"

"Wow," said Doc, astounded that they had travelled to the other side of the world. "I guess not."

"Good. We're ready. Cloak on?"

"Check!" Doc replied, as a sack was thrust into his hands.

"We'll start you off with an easy one," said Alfonso, showing Doc his elfPad.

The picture on the screen could have been from anywhere. It was a traditional Christmas. Sparkling lights outlined the picture window, stockings hung from the mantle and Doc could even make out a glass of milk sitting on a small table beside the fireplace. The only thing that seemed strange was that the entire scene seemed to be viewed from floor level.

Alfonso slowly turned the elfPad to the left, changing the view. It was a live feed, and Doc saw a giant present come into view, along with Christmas lights attached to a low hanging branch at the top of the picture.

Doc pulled back and looked inquisitively at Alfonso.

"Keep looking," he said.

Alfonso swiped a slider on the elfPad and the view zoomed out to include first one window frame, then several others. He turned the elfPad further and Doc saw the plastic interior of a toy train car.

"This is how we've done it, pretty much since model trains were invented," Alfonso explained. "A simple toy train around a Christmas tree, in homes all over the world. Are you ready?"

Doc was still struggling to take everything in, but he nodded anyway.

"Good, you're all set," said Alfonso. "Look at the picture, and go there. When you arrive, get out of the train, get bigger, put the presents under the tree, and then head back."

It sounded simple, Doc thought, as he concentrated on the picture.

* * *

He appeared almost instantly inside the train car. He was right beside the window and promptly lost his balance as the model train car shifted slightly with his weight. He quickly recovered and looked outside. The view was amazing. He was looking at the same scene he'd viewed on the elfPad moments before. He headed for the train car door and hopped down. He looked up at the tree from far below and then a second later he was looking directly at it. He'd hardly thought about growing bigger. He'd simply done it.

Feeling quite proud of himself, Doc looked down at the train car he'd just emerged from. It was just a cheap plastic train, the kind you might find in a dollar store. It was wonderful that even such a train was enough for the magic to work. He then noticed then that he'd dropped the gift bag when he'd lost his balance, so he shrank down and retrieved it. He delivered the gifts then got back in the car.

Doc then realized that he didn't know how to get back. Alfonso hadn't really said anything about that. He closed his eyes and tried thinking about where he'd landed with the team but nothing happened. However, when he opened his eyes, he was back with Alfonso in the Tourist Train way station.

"What? How?"

"Not bad Doc," Alfonso smiled. "We didn't have to come and get you."

"But, well you couldn't have anyway," Doc replied.

"Contagious, remember?"

"Right," agreed Alfonso. "Which is why we started you off in an empty house."

"I don't understand."

"This family are at their grandparents' house and won't be home until mid-morning. We tried to find the safest places to get you each started. Letting you discover is much easier than endless training, which we didn't have the time for anyway. So? Comments? Questions?"

Doc thought for a moment.

"Is there some way I can communicate with you? Should I bring an elfPad?"

Alfonso gestured to one of the other elves who brought over a small case.

"We didn't want to start you off with these, although they are part of your gear."

Alfonso opened the case, nestled inside was a small elfPad on a wrist mount and a pair of Eraylin, the earpieces that the elves loved so much. Alfonso helped Doc put them on.

"You're now linked to all of us via the wrist-rack," he said, showing Doc some basic operation. This controls your ear lights. If you want to show us something, just point at it with your hand. It's a live feed."

"That's it?"

"For now," said Alfonso with a smile. "There are a lot more features and functions that we'll help you with should the need arise. For now, this is probably enough. Ready?

"Yes," Doc said, then added. "No wait! What about the milk and cookies? Don't I have to eat them or something?"

The elves all laughed at that.

"You certainly can if you want to," said Alfonso. "But don't worry, the parents usually take care of that anyway. Otherwise we'd all weigh 500 pounds!"

"Okay," said Doc, as he accepted the next bag of presents. "I'm ready."

"Look on the wrist-rack. It will display the house you're delivering to, and if you need it, it will show you this location so you can get back, in case you get disoriented."

Doc thought that was an odd thing to say, before he looked at the picture on his wrist-rack. It was obviously a different home but still full of Christmas decorations and paraphernalia. However the image was tilted at about a 30-degree angle. He looked at Alfonso in alarm.

"Easy is over," said Alfonso. "It's down to business. These folks don't have a train around the tree. Looks like a train ornament, hanging on a tree."

Doc gritted his teeth and took a deep breath.

"I'm good," he said, and vanished.

* * *

After he had dropped the presents off, Doc flashed back into the ornament somewhere near the middle, lost his balance, then slid ungraciously down to its lower end. He grimaced and flashed himself back to the tourist train way station. He handed Alfonso the empty bag then noticed that all the elves were standing in a row, each one looking at him and holding a bag ready for delivery. "Too slow?" Doc asked.

"Not at all," replied Alfonso. "You're learning and learning quickly."

"But?" asked Doc, looking to the line of elves.

"We want to be ready once you hit your stride," said Alfonso.

"What do you mean."

Alfonso just smiled.

"You'll see."

"Fine," said Doc.

He grabbed the next bag and looked at his wrist. He went through another tree train and made the delivery without any problems.

* * *

Then he did the next one, through a toy train wrapped up as a present. He had to poke a pinhole to be able see where he was going. He then traveled onto a unfinished train layout in the basement of a model railroader's house, followed by a caboose that had been converted to a room at a bed and breakfast, then another tree train.

Doc started to notice that elves were slowing down. He'd soon dealt with the line of bags and they were barely keeping up with him. Concerned, he stopped and turned to Alfonso.

"What's wrong? You guys were so far ahead."

Alfonso grinned excitedly.

"You hit your stride!"

He showed Doc a playback on his elfPad. It showed Doc coming back from the ornament, and getting the next bag. Then the recording seemed to speed up as Doc blurred slightly grabbing another bag. He was back from that delivery in only a few seconds!

"How?" Doc asked.

He said as he watched the next few deliveries get faster and faster until he was just a blur and then things returned to normal and he heard his recorded voice saying. 'What's wrong? You guys were so far ahead?'

They were all beaming at him.

"Magic?" said Doc, although he already knew the answer. "And this is happening to all of us?"

"As we speak," Alfonso confirmed, proudly.

Doc took a deep breath and exhaled slowly as he thought about his family and friends.

"Okay then, let's go!"

* * *

The evening became a blur for all of them. Yet certain trips stood out for each of them and created memories that would last forever.

Ken's team used a bullet train that was sitting idle in its yards in Japan, delivering gifts through in-home train layouts in several nearby cities. Once he even emerged in a music box containing a train! Harry was in his element at the Wensleydale Railway and several others like it in England. He made deliveries through everything from old and dusty three rail attic layouts to Thomas the Tank Engine home sets in children's rooms.

To their delight Vicki and Jeanette found themselves distributing presents from a model of the Disney Monorail in the gift shop of Disney World in Florida. Jeanette stayed back once when they delivered through an eerie, darkened, garden railroad layout, but was happy to help when they delivered to the hospital for sick children. Jeanette even handled a couple of floors by herself. A task made relatively easy since there was a Christmas Tree with a train around it on every floor. She and her mom actually were spotted by sharp eyed kids a few times there, but their Elf-Tec cloak and Jeanette's charm saved the day.

Conductor Ross ended up in Jamaica, in a broken down train that was completely overgrown with plants. On one occasion he really got to run around like Santa Claus, as he delivered to an entire village through a single tree train layout in a church, from there sneaking into each house in the village, one by one.

The always-outspoken Janice was completely tongue-tied when she left her way station in a parked NYC subway car, and traveled onto Rod Stewart's famous *Grand Street & Three Rivers* model train layout to deliver Christmas to the rocker's East Coast home.

Helga thought Fetna was joking when Doc's very own train layout was used as one of their way stations. She also made several trips through the lobby train at the hotel where Nick had been staying - to deliver presents to the guests there. Her favorite though, was a delivery through a ceramic Christmas train that was part of a Christmas Village display. Pierre, Helga's bartender friend, found himself in a creepy streetcar graveyard from where a delivery to the usual train around the tree became unexpectedly exciting when a preset timer took the train, along with Pierre, for a few loops around the tree.

George did very well, but his best deliveries were through somewhere he'd been many times in real life. His favorite way station was the Nevada Northern Railway steam train. It was interesting just how many deliveries from there were through souvenir trains from that very same railway. However his weirdest trip was through a model train stored in a box that was kept at the back of a closet.

All over the world in country after country, presents were successfully delivered. When one way station was empty, the helpers and their elves traveled back to the Pole, then hitched another ride out to the next way station bringing another trainload of presents.

CHAPTER 43

Winding Down

Doc could see that the sun wasn't rising yet but the stars did seem just a little less twinkly when they left the way station at the West Coast Railway Association in British Columbia and flashed back to the North Pole for their next load.

The lines of trains queuing to enter the Hub no longer seemed so endless. A couple of the tracks only had a few smaller trains on them. Without warning, Alfonso and his team promised they'd see Doc later, and before he could ask why, dashed off. Nick came up behind him, caught his elbow and pulled him aside.

"You've done well!" said Nick. "We'll be all done soon. Take a break with me. Vicki and Jeanette will be here shortly."

"Are you sure?" Doc asked.

"Yes, yes," said Nick pointing at the globe. "Not much to do now."

The last zone of really bright lights was slowly dimming and changing color. There were still a few bright lights in the Pacific Ocean and lots left in Alaska but overall the populated areas along the west coast of the USA and Canada were now dimmer than they'd been earlier.

"So how do you deliver to those houses that don't just have trains in them?" Doc asked. "They can't all have trains."

Nick smiled.

"You'd be surprised at how few homes don't have some sort of train in them, but for those we deliver their gifts by sheer Christmas magic. It is our greatest resource, but not one we can serve the whole world with. Look there."

Nick pointed to one of the time zones where the helper team deliveries had been completed. It still showed plenty of destinations, although there were now only thousands, rather than the millions that had been there earlier.

"And there," Nick said, pointing out one special track that had a special hoop portal which a loaded train was slowly approaching.

As the train passed through the portal the normal glow pulsed with independent flickers. Doc watched the train progress through the hoop then he looked up at the globe. The illuminated destinations in the time zone that Nick had pointed out were slowly winking out as the train progressed through the hoop. When the train had cleared the hoop about a third of that time zone was completely dark, all presents had been delivered in that area. Another loaded train was already queued up behind it, waiting to continue the process.

CHAPTER 44

About The Reindeer

Doc followed the progress of the completion of the time zone. Then he noticed that Vicki and Jeanette were standing with Fetna watching from a point further along the platform.

Nick looked over to Cyril who gave him a thumbs up.

"Looks like we'll make it for sure," said Nick. "You, your family, and all your friends have saved Christmas."

"I need some air," he said. "You coming?"

They beckoned Fetna and the girls over. Helga arrived to join them as well. The other helpers that were finished were busy sharing stories on the platforms below.

Nick climbed up a level and headed out the door to the landing platform beside the dome. They looked over the land below. There were empty trains in the yards and a growing number of happy elves filled the streets. Far above them birds circled in the clouds.

Jeanette walked over to Nick.

"I really like the trains, but does that mean the stories about the reindeer aren't true?"

Nick laughed.

"Of course not, my dear! Why, there was a time when we used only reindeer, but the world just got too big."

"Are all the reindeer gone then?" she asked.

Nick laughed again.

"Goodness no!"

He turned and whistled sharply. In the clouds above a portion of the flock of birds veered off and flew down towards them. As they drew closer, they began to assume a familiar formation. Long before they landed, it was easy to see that they were not birds at all, but reindeer! They landed on the roof beside Nick and the others, hoping for a snack, which Fetna was happy to provide.

Nick gave one of the reindeer a scratch between the ears. "Normally I take them out for a few gift runs during the night, but it just wasn't possible this year."

His eyes glinted mischievously.

"I'm feeling a bit better now. Maybe I can give you a ride home in the old sleigh?"

"Wow!" said Vicki, in amazement.

"Thanks!" Jeanette exclaimed, although she was much cooler about it than her mom.

Fetna didn't say anything. He and Helga were listening, but were also holding hands as if they were schoolyard crushes.

Nick smiled at them, then looked over at Doc, who was shaking his head.

"Still don't believe Doc?"

"No, it's not that. I was just thinking about the last few years since Marilee passed."

"I believe she'd be very proud of you right now," said Nick.

"I know she would, Dad," Vicki added. "You always fix everything, even Christmas when it was sick!"

"Grandpa," said Jeanette. "You're Doc Christmas!"

"Doc Christmas! I like that!" said Nick, laughing heartily.

Doc was smothered in a family hug. The reindeer took off and performed a few circles in the sky, in celebration of a special day well done.

ME, YOU and the REVIEW

Thanks for reading this book. I hope you enjoyed it as much as I enjoyed writing it! If you did, then I've got some great news for you... Doc Christmas is headed for the big screen. We don;t know where or when

If you want advance news on the movie, or next book in the series, the best way to get it is to sign up for my email newsletter at **neilenock.com.**

If you want more than just advance news, well, that's going to cost you! Okay, not really, but there is something that **only you** can do, that will help it get done sooner. Write a review!

First, book reviews let you share your thoughts and feelings about a book, and lets the rest of the world know that there are people out there reading the book!

Second, indie authors especially depend on reviews. Without enough reviews, we are often excluded from marketing and promotional opportunities.

So, If you have an opportunity, I would greatly appreciate it if you could write a review.

Thanks,
Neil

P.S. If you don't know how to write a review...
itinkr.com/couldnt-put-that-book-down
And you can post a review at goodreads.com, amazon.com, my website or almost any bookseller!

ABOUT THE AUTHOR

Most of my stories have come to me first as screenplays. People often tell me they can see the movie in their head when they read the book. I haven't yet figured out if that's a bad thing or a good thing, so I'll probably just keep going until I do.

When I'm not writing, I keep pretty busy with filmaking and related storytelling projects in Calgary - usually with some or all of my family on tow.

I write the occasional blog post at **NeilEnock.com**
Join me on Twitter **@NeilEnock** on
Facebook at **NeilEnock**
or there's always the standards...
www.neilenock.com   **neil@itinkr.com**

AN EPIC SCI-FI ADVENTURE

Mayan is an astonishing history lesson embedded in a satisfying thriller worthy of James Rollins or Spielberg
            - Patrick Nichol, Chapters.Indigo.ca

More that 5,000 years after they began planning for their voyage, the Mayan & Minoan ship Atlantis returns to recolonize the world, after skipping 'the end' in 2012. There's just one small problem...

                    ... we're still here!

• Will Atlantis' 5 millennia journey be brought to an abrupt end?
• Can the past and the present be united to save the future?

MAYAN - Atlantis Returns

ISBN 978-1-988108-01-8 (paperbook)
ISBN 978-1-988108-03-2 (electronic)

Cover Photography: Neil Speers & Neil Enock
Models: Victoria Souter and Neil Enock
Train Layout: Osoyoos Desert Model Railway
Hardcover Foil Art: Matthew Stewart
Cover Design: Neil Speers & iTinkr Studios

www.ingramcontent.com/pod-product-compliance
Lightning Source LLC
Chambersburg PA
CBHW051341020726
47501CB00007B/2203